CONSEQUENCES

By

Mary Kay

Published by New Generation Publishing in 2017

Copyright © Mary Kay 2017

First Edition

The author asserts the moral right under the Copyright, Designs and Patents Act 1988 to be identified as the author of this work.

All Rights reserved. No part of this publication may be reproduced, stored in a retrieval system or transmitted, in any form or by any means without the prior consent of the author, nor be otherwise circulated in any form of binding or cover other than that which it is published and without a similar condition being imposed on the subsequent purchaser.

www.newgeneration-publishing.com

 New Generation Publishing

Also by this author

Sooner or Later

9781787191686

2016

CHAPTER ONE

Unknown to their parents, teenagers, Molly and Pippa, had gone in for a competition. The prize, if they won, would be a weekend at a Skiing Resort. They guessed that their parents wouldn't let them go even if they did win, but were sure that somehow they would be able to get their own way. Each morning they watched for the post, and at last their patience was rewarded. Pippa ran out to collect the letters from the mailbox in front of the house, and seeing one that had her sister's name on the envelope, she stuffed it into the pocket of her jeans and took the remainder indoors to place on the breakfast table. Murmuring to Molly as she did so. You've got a letter. Molly choked on her juice, but at Pippa's frown and headshake, she repressed the words she had been about to shriek. At last they escaped and were on their way to High School. Pippa pulled out the letter, and Molly opened it with trembling hands, and with Pippa looking over her shoulder she read…. Miss Molly Manning has won a voucher for a weekend for two at the Snow World Resort. Gee it's so exciting Pippa exclaimed what are we going to wear, shall we get some new outfits. First of all we have to find out if Mom and Dad will let us go, Molly cautioned her sister. Sure they will Pippa replied, why wouldn't they? Because they'll say we're too young and irresponsible. Molly said. You know what they're like. They always say the same thing, and that's No! She said. We could ask them to come with us, Pippa suggested. Molly laughed, Can you see Mom on Ski's? She grinned, and Dad's always too busy. If Gil were here I guess he would come, but he's in Ottawa on business and that only leaves Fern and I don't suppose she would want to come either. Molly replied. Perhaps we could just go and not tell Mom, you know, just leave a note, but not say exactly where we're going. Pippa suggested. Yeah, great! And have half the police in the County looking for us, I don't think so. Her sister replied. That's it then, Pippa said gloomily. Then never one to give up easily she said. But what if we asked Mom and Dad and see what they say? This course of action was agreed and they hurried their steps and were only just in time to catch the school bus.

When the girls arrived home from school that afternoon, they found Fern sitting in the kitchen talking to their Mother, who was ironing. The girls had agreed to face their Mother together with their proposition, and although Fern was there they didn't mind for most of the time she understood their point of view. She was still young enough to remember her school days vividly, and how often she had been barred from doing the things that the other girls were allowed to do. This time however she took no part in the argument that raged in the kitchen. Dora claimed that it had been an underhand act on Molly's part to apply for the competition without her parent's permission. And the girls argued that they were never allowed to do anything interesting.

The reason why we have to curb your high jinks is because you never think before you act, and that puts you and others at risk. Dora said. You are like a pair of loose cannons sometimes; we never know what you are going to do next. And this has proved us right again. The girls stomped upstairs and slammed their bedroom doors.

Whew! Fern exclaimed. That was some 'Statement'. Yes and it will probably get worse before it gets better, Dora laughed. Welcome to your first family row.

Fern thought for a moment, then she said tentatively, I don't want to interfere, but supposing I were to go with them, would that help? It seems a shame to disappoint them when they were so delighted with their win. Dora looked doubtful, can you ski? She asked. Well, actually no I can't, but I only need to be the adult present, they can learn to ski and I can just keep an eye on them. How hard can that be? Fern replied.

I'll see what Phil says tonight, we won't say anything to the girls just yet; we'll play it by ear and see how it goes. Dora decided.

After the girls had gone to bed Dora and Phil discussed the matter, and Dora told him of Fern's offer to go with the girls as a chaperone. I don't know if it's a good idea Honey, Fern's only a kid herself, would she be able to control those two, they're a pretty strong force when they both get together on something. After some more discussion and the assurance from the girls that they would do exactly as Fern told them to do, it was at last agree, and the offer was accepted. There was one fault in the plan, for during the discussions, nobody had thought to call Fern's husband Gil and include him in their decision

Fern hoped that she had made the right decision to go with the girls. It's too late now she told herself, and so she packed a bag with warm clothes and one dress just in case she needed to dress up more in the dining room. The girl's packing was not so simple and nearly drove their mother demented. They finally ended with three large holdalls each, so that Dora had to take charge, and in spite of their repeated objections she managed to reduce them down to one bag each.

Dora and Phil drove them to the meeting place, where they met the bus that would take them to the Ski Resort. And so with hugs and kisses and many last minute warnings and instructions they were on their way.

Phew! I thought we'd never get here gasped Pippa, as she settled comfortably in her seat. Fern sat across the aisle from them, next to a pleasant middle-aged lady. She and Fern soon set up a conversation. Fern told her of the girls win and why she was coming with them, and Iris explained that she was a widow, and had decided that she was going to do all the things she had not been able to do when young. Well most of them anyway she added with a laugh

During the journey most people slept or watched the TV screen, wearing the earphones supplied. It was dark when they arrived at the Resort and everyone tumbled out of the Bus glad to stretch their legs. A Buffet Meal was provided and then they went to the wardrobe to be fitted with ski clothing. After that they were free to go to bed or watch TV in their rooms. Fern and the girls were glad to have a shower and go to bed for it had been a long day. And the breakfast call was at 7 30am.the next morning.

The next morning found the girls out on the ski slopes directly after breakfast. Neither of them were good skiers. Fern didn't ski at all, but she was happy to watch the girls as they slipped and tumble and laughed. The Ski instructor was a handsome young man and all the girls flocked around him, Molly and Pippa declared that he was a 'Dream Boat' but soon lost interest in him and wanted to go to the higher mountain slopes. I don't' think you're strong enough skiers to go up there Fern cautioned them. Oh we don't want to ski, we want to look at the view and take some photos. Fern agreed and they seated themselves in a three-seated chair. As the chair lift rose higher, the girls were delighted and leaned over the sides taking pictures and making the chair swing about. Fern was extremely nervous of heights and felt as if she were being drawn down the mountainside, she held the side of the chair so tightly that her knuckles were white and he arms began to ache. She was thankful when they reached the platform at the top where they disembarked. The girls both jumped out of the chair and without waiting for Fern and ran towards the little Café. Fortunately the attendant at the top helped Fern out of the chair and after thanking him she followed the two girls to the Café. Feeling that she needed a cup of strong coffee to settle her nerves.

While they were in the Café, the sky, which had been Blue, had now become overcast and a few flakes of snow had begun to fall. He girls were tired of taking photos and wanted to go higher up the slopes. I don't think that's a good idea, Fern cautioned them. The weather looks as if it might take a turn for the worst and we'll be caught up there. It won't be long before the ski lift will stop if the weather gets bad, and we'll be stranded. I think we should go down now. But the girls were already out of earshot, they had forgotten their promise to do as Fern directed and as usual had gone their own way.

Fern was in a quandary. Should she wait until they came down again, or should she go after them? In the end she decided to follow them, she preferred to know what they were doing rather than wait there and worry. She began to follow the path that the girls had taken, it was hard work for it was two steps forward and one step back for the snow was icy hard. After what seemed like hours she heard their voices and they were coming back much to Fern's relief. When they neared the return platform, the Chair lift was about to leave, and the three girls had to run the last few yards on the slippery snow. Suddenly Fern's feet sipped from under her and she began to fall down the last 100 yards over and over she fell, she couldn't stop her self, the girls were frozen in shock, but could do nothing to help her they were too far behind her. At last Fern did stop, when she landed with a resounding 'Crash' head first against the metal edge of the landing stage. She lay in the snow, twisted and still with blood pouring from her head. For a second nobody moved and then the attendant barked at the girls, 'Go into the Café and tell the woman to ring the Mountain Rescue Team, tell them that it's urgent'. Meanwhile he was taking off his muffler and binding it around Fern's head trying to stem the flow of blood. Fern was air lifted to hospital, while the girls had the unenviable job of ringing their parents to tell them what had happened.

Dora and Phil came at once; the girls dreaded their arrival for they knew that they were going to be in 'Big Trouble' to put it mildly. At the hospital the news was not good. Fern had serious head injuries, multiple bruising and abrasions. And she was unconscious. Both of the girls were in trouble with their parents, who were furious and told hem how disappointed they were with them after they had trusted them to go away with Fern. Now look at the consequences of your selfish disobedience. I dread to think what Gil is going to say. I had to call and tell him. He was in a meeting but I'm expecting to hear from him at any moment. You are both going to wish you hadn't been born when you hear his fury. It's going to be bad I can tell you, and don't expect any help or sympathy from your father and me for you have really run your length this time and now after repeated warnings you are going to get what you deserve.

Fern could hear quiet voices, she listened for a while, who were they? Somebody seemed to be discussing a problem that they were trying to solve. Gradually she drifted into a natural sleep, thinking. I'm too tired to bother about that now. The nurse, who had been sitting beside her bed, had seen her move and open her eyes for a moment before she had slept. She took Fern's pulse and checked the machinery beside her bed, then quickly went to find the Sister and report that Mrs. Manning had roused from her Coma and was now in a natural sleep. More OBS were taken and her notes discussed. This is hopeful the Doctor observed. Let me know at once if there is any more progress. I'm concerned about any brain damage.

Once more Fern woke; she looked around the room, immediately the nurse was at her side. Would you like a drink she asked.. What about a nice cup of tea? I'd love one thank you Fern replied. When the nurse brought the tea, she asked do you take sugar? Fern opened her mouth to answer, but couldn't remember whether she had sugar in her tea or not. She dismissed the puzzle for the moment. Because the nurse was saying your Husband will be so relieved and delighted when he finds that you have woken from your coma. Fern frowned. What husband? She thought. I don't remember any husband. Presently a doctor came to see her. He asked her several questions, which she was unable to answer, and she was beginning to get worried. The doctor was very concerned too, and he called his colleagues to a meeting. After giving Fern tests it was confirmed that she was suffering from Amnesia.

The repercussions in the family were great. Gil especially was bitterly angry with his sisters, and could hardly bear to speak to them. He would often leave the room if they were present. At first Fern was bewildered, but she soon began to accept her disability, and carried a note book with her so that she could jot down each new memory that she had re-learned about herself, the family and friends.

Eventually in desperation Gil decided to take Fern to England to see if her childhood home would help her regain her memory.

CHAPTER TWO

Tessa and Bart, their friends, when asked were both delighted to have Fern with them and hoped that it would help her to regain her memory. Fern's Goddaughter Marina was now a toddler and they had a new baby, Jamie.

When Fern and Gil arrived there was so much news to catch up, and the new baby to admire. Marina had been a baby when Fern left for Canada, but she was soon chatting as if she has known Fern forever. The biggest surprise was Fern's dog Bitza. When Gil and Fern arrived, Bart was out taking Bitza for his daily walk. When they returned Bitza recognised Fern, and ran to her, jumping up and trying to lick her face, and to Gil's delight Fern fell to her knees hugging him and letting him lick her chin saying. Darling Bitza, I've missed you so much. For a moment nobody spoke and then everyone was talking at once.

Once the children were in bed, the adults were able to discuss Fern's loss of memory. I'm hoping that seeing old friends and places will help Fern, Gil explained. It's worth a try Tessa said after all just remembering Bitza was a step forward and we'll help all we can, but where will you start? I was thinking of beginning by going to visit Fern's old college friends. And perhaps taking her back to East Leigh, but Fern isn't keen on going there. Not since you've told me that I wasn't happy there, Fern complained.

The next day Gil began to ring Fern's College friends, and made arrangements to meet them.

First they went to visit Ziggy, who worked as a jewellery designer in London. Fern felt foolish. What if Ziggy thought that she was making a fuss over nothing? But she need not have worried, for Ziggy was sympathetic and delighted to help her and tell her about their student days and other friends. But Fern didn't remember, which saddened Ziggy, for she knew that Gil had hoped for a result. Their next visit was to Libby, who was married to the son of the Gallery owner who had been her Boss. She admired Libby's paintings, which were mostly modernist. But she had no memory of them either. Their next visit was to Mrs.Myers Hostel where the girls had lodged, Mrs.Myers was delighted to see them, for she liked to keep track of any of her lodgers who had been successful, and she considered Fern one of the most successful because she was married to the Author of popular detective novels. Through all these visits Fern couldn't remember anyone or anything that the girls had mentioned. Not even Smitty, who had been a particular friend and had been best man at her wedding. Fern was beginning to get distressed, and Gil judged it time to give up for the moment and return to Hampstead.

Fern found Marina and baby Jamie a great comfort. For her loss of memory was weighing heavily on her and she had begun to think that Gil was getting tired of her. But actually, he was giving her some space for he felt that he was been pressing her too much to remember her past, so that she had become quiet and withdrawn. Gil decided that he would rent the beach cottage where he had stayed when he first met Fern. And so they departed for Eastleigh with the hope that a visit there would help to bring back any memories of her past.

Tessa was sitting at the kitchen table making her shopping list, when Marina came in from the garden announcing; Mummy there's a baby in he shed. Yes darling, Tessa said absently, wondering to herself how many potatoes to order. I think its hungry, persisted Marina. Tessa looked up. Where did it come from? She asked.

I think the Angels put it there, it's a baby angel, but it hasn't got any wings yet. Marina replied. Can we keep it and can I give it one of Jamie's bottles? She clambered onto a chair and leant her elbows on the table. Can I give it one of Jamie's bottles? She persisted. Tessa gave up trying to concentrate on her shopping list, and gave in to the

Pester Power of her daughter. Come and look. Marina insisted.

With a sigh, and knowing she would get no peace until she went out into the garden. Tessa rose from her seat and followed her daughter. Marina skipped along the garden path, ahead of her mother; and opened the door of the shed. Tessa was about to join in Marina's fantasy, but the words died on her lips, for there, lying on an old blanket in the wheel barrow was a real baby. It lay sleeping peacefully, and with its sweet little face and dusting of golden hair it really did look like a little angel. Tessa looked around and saw evidence of habitation, and then she picked up the baby and carried it into the house.

The baby was very wet, and there were no nappies amongst the meagre supply of clothing and toiletries in the battered little bag that had been beside the garden lounger, where somebody had obviously been sleeping. Tessa took a nappy from her own Baby Bag. The baby slept on undisturbed by the nappy changing.

I wish Jamie were such a sound sleeper, Tessa thought, as she laid the baby in the carrycot that she kept for convenience in the kitchen. Her first thought was to phone the police. But on reflection decided to wait and see if the mother came back .She would like to hear her side of the situation before she acted. The baby slept on peacefully, watched over by an attentive Marina, who claimed that it was her own Baby Angel.

Tessa was beginning to wonder if she should now phone the police, when there was a tap on the back door. On the doorstep stood a young girl. She was poorly dressed and looked ill. Tessa opened the door wider and ushered her into the kitchen, saying kindly, Come in and sit down, I'll put the kettle on and you can tell me why you're living in my shed. I'm Tessa Reece. What's your name? The girl was at first reluctant to open up and tell Tessa her name and her reason for being a down and out,, but at last encouraged by Tessa's kindness she told her story.

Lisa's parents held very strict views, especially her Father, who thought that she should be governed by him, because she was only seventeen and under age. This had not bothered Lisa very much, for she was not of a rebellious nature. That was until she met Jason. His family had recently moved into the new houses that had been built in the village and with him came new ideas. She was a pretty little girl but rather shy. Jason was attracted to her for that reason. He was tired of the fast flashy girls who flocked around him for his good looks and money. Lisa was his ideal, but he couldn't get near her, she seemed to have an invisible wall around her, a space that nobody could enter, and she seemed oblivious to his existence. But Lisa had noticed the tall handsome Jason, who was pursued by all the other girls, and she made sure to keep well away, for she knew how much her parents would disapprove of him.

Fate however decided otherwise, for one very wet afternoon as she cycled home from school a car swished by her and drenched her with water from a huge puddle in the dip of the road. She overbalanced and fell off her cycle. Soaked and badly shaken, Lisa sat in the road and burst into tears. The driver jumped from his vehicle and rushed to help her, apologising profusely as he did so. Where do you live? He asked. I'll take you home and come back for your cycle later. I'm Jason Clarke by the way, and you're Lisa aren't you? How do you know who I am? Lisa asked momentarily diverted from her wet state. Oh I know more than you think, he replied. And I like what I know. I've wanted to get to know you for ages, but could never seem to get near you as you always disappear before I get the chance. Will you come out with me on a date? Certainly not! Lisa declared, I don't know you let alone like you. Please take me straight home and we'll forget this ever happened.

When the car drew up outside her home Lisa slid quickly from her seat, ran along the garden path to the door, and disappeared without a backward glance. Jason sighed. Well Mate, he told himself, this is going to be a long haul but it'll be worth it in the end. She's the girl for me. I know it, but it seems that she doesn't feel the same. Well nothing venture nothing gain, I'm not giving up yet.

Unknown to Jason, Lisa was very attracted to him. She set her mind against the attraction, because she was so used to being dictated to by her father that she had lost the will to do otherwise. Whenever she saw Jason in the distance she would deliberately go in another direction, at one time she had even hidden behind a skip. At last she became so tired of this 'Cat and mouse' game, she felt that she must confront Jason and set the boundaries. And so one afternoon when she saw him coming towards her, instead of disappearing as usual she confronted him. Will you please stop following me wherever I go? She demanded. It makes me feel as if I'm being stalked, and it's very disconcerting. I'm trying to get to know you, but you keep disappearing like a 'Wil-O-The Wisp' I don't have the plague you know and I'm quite harmless, you might even get to like me if you stay sill long enough to find out. Jason replied. Lisa looked at him steadily for a moment. Why would you want to know me? She asked. Jason shook his head and smiled. What a prickly little hedgehog you are he joked. What can I say? I'm the friendly type; I like to be friendly with everyone, and you look like a nice girl, not like some of these fast floosies who think of nothing but running after men just to get a good time.

Lisa was surprised, she had always been given to understand that was what most young men wanted, but it seemed that here was one young man who was different, her attitude towards him softened, and unknown to her parents she began to meet and go out with Jason. Her parents thought that she was staying on later at school for extra tutoring, or to do her homework and Lisa wrongly let them think this. It was only a matter of time before things became out of hand.

Jason was now deeply in love with Lisa. He was twenty-two, and when he discovered that she was only seventeen and still at school, he was shocked, for she behave in such a mature manner that she appeared older. Lisa not knowing that Jason was in love with her continued in her dream world, hoping that one-day Jason would feel the same as her. Once more fate took a hand, for one evening after a hot sunny day, Lisa and Jason met and decided to go for a walk in the woods. It was cool under the trees and after they had walked for a while they sat beneath a large tree, to rest and talk before returning home. Lisa Lay back amongst the grass and leaves looking up at the leafy branches above, while Jason leaned against the tree trunk, gazing at Lisa wishing that he had the nerve to make love to her. Something fell from the tree and landed on Lisa's neck, She shrieked and went into a panic, flapping her hands against herself thinking it had gone down into her clothing. Jason jumped up and began to help her strip off her T-shirt, all the while Lisa was sobbing, for she had a phobia about biting insects, especially spiders. Jason was trying to help her and then one thing led to another and they both lost their heads. Afterwards they lay in the grass together and realised what they had done, both fervently hoping that there would be no consequences. But of course as the saying goes 'Take what you want sayeth the Lord. And Pay for it.'

CHAPTER THREE

Life went on as usual and Lisa saw little of Jason, for he had gone away on a course to do with his job. Before he went he gave her his number, and made her promise to let him know if all was well. Later when she did phone him, she was told that he wasn't available, having been sent away unexpectedly to another job.

Lisa sat for a moment with the phone still in her hand. Then she let it fall back into its cradle. Her stomach was turning over and over and suddenly she ran for the bathroom reaching it just in time. She sat in the bathroom for a while with no idea what she was going to do. Then she went into her bedroom and began to pack a small holdall. She collected all the loose money that she had, and her savings book. Her parents were both at work, and so leaving a short note for them; she went to the station and caught a train to London.

It was a big bewildering place and seemed to be crowded with people and traffic. Does nobody ever sleep here she wondered? The evening grew later and still there was no sign of stillness. After midnight it seemed a little calmer and then she began to see bodies lying in corners or in any convenient place. I suppose they are what the papers call 'Rough Sleepers' She told herself. I never thought that I would ever become one of them. She walked along beside the river and seeing a space on one of the benches she sat down wearily. Her belongings clutched tightly to her chest. She must have dozed off for she was suddenly aware of someone trying to drag away her bag, I was twisted about her arms and couldn't be taken.' Get off me' she shrieked kicking the person vigorously in the shins. Swearing and a cuff round the head followed, but Lisa still held fast to her bag. 'Give it 'ere'. Growled a gruff voice. 'No' shrieked Lisa it's mine. Goodness knows what the outcome would have been if a third party hadn't intervened.

Luckily a man in uniform had come to her aid. Lisa thought that she recognised the uniform. When the man explained that he was from the Salvation Army, and was doing his rounds for the night, looking for vulnerable young people who needed a meal and a bed, she felt relieved that here was someone reliable who would help her. She followed him to the nearest shelter and after filling a form and being questioned, she was given a meal and a bed for the night. I don't know what I'm going to do tomorrow she thought as she lay down and instantly fell into an exhausted sleep.

In the morning she washed and tidied herself as best she could and went into the Dining Hall. She ate a good breakfast and was then directed to the Office where the Captain was working on some papers. He picked up Lisa's form. I see that you're only seventeen, he said, looking at her over the top of his spectacles. What's a young lady your age doing here, and do your parents know where you are? He asked. Lisa looked down at the toes of her shoes and shook her head. The Captain looked at her respectable clothes and shoes, and made a calculation. So I must suppose that you've run away from home and feel that you can't go back.

Were you ill treated? Lisa shook her head. Did you have an argument with your parents? Another shake of the head greeted this question. Then why did you run away? Asked the puzzled Captain. Because I'm Pregnant. Was the sobbed reply, and I can't tell them, my Dad will kill me. We could send someone with you to explain to him. The Captain offered. Lisa shook her head, what about after you'd gone? They would still be able to punish me. She said. What does the baby's father say, is he willing to be helpful? I tried to get in touch with him, but he's working away and I don't know where he is. Well, if you really don't want to go home we can get you into a Hostel until you've had the baby. The Captain replied. Lisa agreed, and the Captain assured her that he would make arrangements for her, but urged her to tell her parents once she was settled.

At the Hostel she became friendly with another girl, named Brenda. But most people call me Bren she introduced herself. Her baby was due about the same time as Lisa's. Eventually they both had their babies

Bren had a boy and Lisa a girl. Bren's boy friend had been located and had come to visit, they had become reconciled and she was going back to live with him. When at last Lisa had allowed her parents to be contacted, they agreed to take her home, but only if she gave the baby up for adoption. Lisa flatly refused and so there was an impasse, for neither side would change. They were still not able to find the whereabouts of Jason. He no longer worked for the same Company, and nobody knew where he now worked. Jason had once rung Lisa's parents and left a number, asking them to get Lisa to ring him. But of course they never passed the number on to their daughter.

Once the baby was six weeks old Lisa had to leave the Hostel but unlike Bren, she had no boyfriend to help her and so unless she gave in to her parent's ultimatum, she was on her own. She tried to get a job, but couldn't earn enough to live and pay for childcare. She had tried to get Social Security, but she didn't have an address and so was not able to obtain it. She managed to live by staying in various Squats, but by now her small amount of savings were getting low and she was feeling desperate. Someone had told her that Hampstead being an affluent area was a good place to beg, and thus she had arrived in Hampstead. But there were no Squats in Hampstead and so she had devised the idea of Squatting in peoples garden sheds. Tessa's shed was the third one she had used, and now she would have to move on.

Tessa listened to Lisa's story with growing sympathy and when she had finished Tessa said impulsively, you could stay here. We have some attic bedrooms, and maybe you could do some household chores in lieu of rent. If you have an address you will be able to apply for Social

Security for Baby and yourself. Lisa began to look more cheerful and gratefully accepted a mug of tea from Tessa. Meanwhile Marina had been sitting beside the carrycot admiring the baby and dangling toys for her to look at. The baby smiled and gurgled happily. Presently there was the sound of cries from the Baby Minder microphone. That sounds like Master Jamie, Tessa said. I'll just go up and bring him down. When she returned she held the now smiling Jamie in her arms. Oh he's a beautiful boy, Lisa exclaimed, we think so Tessa laughed but we're his family. Your little girl is a real little charmer too. You never told us her name. It's Angela, Lisa replied. Tessa laughed, Marina thought she was a baby Angel when she found her in the shed, and she certainly looks like one with her blue eyes and golden hair. She looks like her Daddy, Lisa said sadly, but I don't suppose he'll ever see her. Don't despair I'm sure we'll manage to find him before too long. Tessa comforted her.

If you've finished your tea, would you like to come up and see the bedroom where you'll sleep?

She carried Jamie and followed by Marina, Lisa and baby Angela, Tessa led the way upstairs. When Bart arrived home, an excited Marina greeted him, telling him that she had found a baby Angel in the shed and that they were going to keep her. But when all was explained he was in full agreement with their decision, and soon they all sat down to their evening meal in great harmony with each other.

Tessa was determined to trace the baby's father. She knew that his name was Jason Clarke, and she knew the name of his last place of work, surely it shouldn't be too hard to trace him.

When Bart came home from work the next day, Tessa asked him 'How do you find people who are missing?

I should imagine going to the police would be the first option. Why do you ask? He replied. Because I want to help Lisa find her baby's father. Tessa said. Firstly I think you should ask Lisa if she wants to find the baby's father.

Bart cautioned, she might look on such an action as interfering.

Lisa when asked if she would like them to try and help her was pleased. Will it cost a lot of money? She asked doubtfully, I don't have much, although I have been trying to save a little. Tessa assured her that it wouldn't cost money only time and patience, and we have plenty of that don't we? When Tessa asked the police about the task of finding Jason, she was told it was classed as a Paternity Case and didn't come under their jurisdiction. Tessa was disappointed but still determined to carry on the search. Bart teased her, you were just the same when we first met and I was crippled, you were so determined that I should walk again, that your urging gave me the will to overcome my difficulties. Don't despair darling if anyone can find Jason it will be you.

One afternoon, Tessa and Lisa sat down together with the telephone on the table, determined to begin their search in earnest. Now I have made a list Tessa said. I have asked the police for help, but that isn't available and so I can tick them off. The next port of call is Jason's old firm. She rang the number that Jason had left with Lisa, and received the same answer they had given Lisa. Jason had left and had mentioned that he was thinking of going abroad to work. We can tick that off the list then. Tessa said. Lisa began to cry. We shall never find him now, she sobbed. Tessa put another tick on her list. Don't be so faint hearted, she chided, we're not giving up yet, not until we've tried every opportunity open. Give me your parent's number she said. They might have a number for him. Even if they do have one, they won't tell us, they hate him and don't want me to find him. Lisa sobbed. Trust me, I've got a few tricks up my sleeve yet, Tessa replied, and she proceeded to ring the number Lisa had just given her. When a woman's voice curtly answered the call, Tessa adopted a false flirty American voice similar to those she had heard in films, when representing a cheap Vamp. Oh, Hi Ma''m! Do I have the right number for Jacey Clarke?

Who are you? Demanded Lillian Glebe. Jacey gave me this number in case I needed to speak with him. I'm Lola D'Vine, drawled Tessa. I sure hope you can put me in touch with Jacey, I'm expecting his baby; He's left me the Rat, and I don't know where he is. My Pa sure wants to get a hold of him and make sure he does the right thing by me and marries me. I'd sure be grateful if you could give me his number so we could catch up with him. Do you mean Jason Clarke, a tall man with Blonde hair, about twenty-two years old? Lillian asked her. Yeah sure, that's him. My Pa'll be grateful and so will I if you can help us.

Lillian Glebe couldn't believe her luck, here was a way to get rid of Jason Clarke forever and teach him a lesson not to seduce young girls ever again. No doubt Lola's 'Pa' would make quite sure that Jason was never again able to stray away, and her own daughter would have to give up her child and return home, for without support she would not be able to manage. She gladly gave Tessa the phone number and any other information that she had and ended the call well pleased with herself. But not as well pleased as Tessa. When she replaced the receiver she punched the air and cheered. 'Bingo! Just like taking candy from a baby. She gloated. She couldn't give me the information fast enough when she thought it would make Jason unobtainable to you.

I don't know when I've enjoyed anything half so much as foiling your Mother's plans.

Where did you learn to act a part so well? Lisa asked. Oh, when I was young I went to Drama College. But after a while, I decided that the Stage was not for me and changed to Art. If I hadn't done so I would never have met Bart, so it must have been meant to happen, or perhaps it was fate.

He said something about being a cripple when he first met you. Lisa said. Yes, he had a bad accident and was very depressed, and had given up trying. Tessa replied. I'm afraid I was determined that he would snap out of it and try to recover. My ultimatum worked. After a great deal of effort he managed it.

Have you known Fern for a long time too? Lisa asked. Yes she was one of my Art Pupils, and she is very talented. It's so sad that she's lost her memory, through an accident. Tessa told her. Will she recover? Lisa asked.

Nobody knows, Tessa replied, but we keep hoping that something will trigger a memory somewhere.

Fern's husband is one of Bart's oldest friends, and was a great support emotionally when Bart's little girl was killed in the same car accident that crippled him. The portrait in the sitting room is of Marietta the other as you can see is one that Bart painted recently of Marina and Jamie. We have to send Marietta's portrait to the picture framers, I'm afraid the frame was damaged during some recent decorating.

Where is Marietta's mother now, did she die in the accident too? Lisa asked. No she left and returned to her family in Italy. She was never strong and she went into a decline and died. Her family blamed Bart for the accident, but it was caused by a huge lorry that 'Jack-knifed' on the motorway and crushed Bart's car. Marietta was killed and Bart was critically injured. It took him several years to get over the tragedy. How awful Lisa sympathised, I don't know if I could ever get over such a dreadful experience.

When Gil first brought Fern to meet Bart, he asked her if he could paint her and they became good friends, so that when Fern came to London and she couldn't bring Bitza, Bart offered to have him here, It was one of the best ideas he could have had, for Bitza is such a good natured little dog, and Bart couldn't resist taking him out on the Heath. Bart was in an electric wheel chair, and up until then wouldn't leave the house. Tessa said.

Gil and Fern are away at the moment. Tessa continued. Fern had an accident and has lost her memory. Gil thought that taking her back to her childhood home might stir some memories. But apparently she had an extremely unhappy time there, so I wouldn't think she would want to remember. But the brain is a complicated organ and nobody really understands it not even the experts, although we can always hope for a miracle. Gil, Fern's husband was a great help to Bart, and that was how he met me. Fern asked Bart if she could bring a friend here to paint the scenery and I was the friend Tessa finished. . Oh it's so romantic it's like a fairy story, Lisa sighed.. It wasn't at first I can tell you Tessa said. Bart was angry with himself for falling in love with me when he was a cripple and had no business to expect a girl to tie herself to him in his condition. What did you do? Lisa asked fascinated by the unfolding of the tale. Tessa smiled, I'm afraid that I became very cross with his defeatist attitude, I lost my temper and told him quite a few 'Home truths' about his attitude. Quite a few more 'Home truths' were exchanged, but it riled Bart up into being determined that he would prove me wrong about him. Sometime losing your temper can bring about good consequences. But losing your temper is not something I would normally recommend, she added with a smile.

Did Bart live in this big house all alone? Lisa asked. Oh no. Tessa replied. He had Mr Stanley to take care for him. He had been Bart's 'Nanny' ever since he left the nursery. His parents were wealthy and once they had a son and heir, they weren't interested in any more children, and spent much of their time travelling abroad. They put Bart into boarding school at five years old, but Mr.Stanley stayed to care for him when he was at home. From what I can gather he was a very lonely little boy, and that was why he began to draw and paint. To give his parents their due, when they discovered how talented Bart was they sent him to the appropriate school to study Art.

He met Maria at the Art School, she was not really very good at Art, but she liked to think that she was. Her father was paying the fees, and so why would the school reject her? She apparently took a fancy to Bart and made up her mind that she would marry him. Bart was not used to young girls, and especially not one as calculating as Maria.

She perused him relentlessly, until he was sure that he must be in love with her, when no doubt he was flattered, for she was popular with the boys, as a flirt, and also because she had a rich father. Her family bounced Bart into marriage. For a short while things were fairly calm, except for the occasional tantrum that vanished as soon she was given her own way. I don't think you could say that Bart was unhappy, but he certainly wasn't content. The worst tantrum of all came when Maria discovered that she was pregnant, and of course she blamed Bart for that. She made everyone's life a misery with her complaining and whining. When Marietta was born she rejected her because she was not a boy. Bart adored the baby, and poured all his love onto her for nobody else seemed to want it. When Marietta was killed in the road accident, Maria blamed Bart and he almost began to believe that it was actually his fault for taking her with him in the car. Matters came to a head when in one of her tantrums Maria decided to leave Bart and to go home to Italy. I think it was a relief to everyone when she went, but it left Bart loaded with guilt about the whole situation. He suffered with depressions for years until I cam on the scene. I'm afraid that I was rather unsympathetic about Maria, but I was determined to help Bart, for I had fallen in love with him, and I knew that he felt the same but wouldn't allow himself to admit it. It took a while but eventually I did convince him, and the rest as they say is history. Maria died young, they said that she went into a decline, but I think that she had actually got into bad company, and was using drugs, with the obvious results.

Mr Stanley is a, dear old chap; He retired when Bart and I were married, and has gone to live with his sister in Guildford. He never married, his fiancé died in a Polio epidemic years ago, and Bart took the place of any child he might have had. That's so sad Lisa said. But it all had a happy ending just as a 'Fairy Tale' should. She sighed.

CHAPTER FOUR

Tessa looked at the clock. If Jason has gone abroad, I'm guessing it will be Canada or America. This is a mobile number so it could be anywhere. We'll wait until its morning in either if those countries. Then we'll see what happens. In the meantime let's go out and get a baby buggy for Angela.

Because the babies were so small they managed to pack them both into Jamie's buggy. It was only a short distance to the shops and so they set out happily, with the two babies and Marina on the footstep at the back of the buggy. My goodness I wouldn't want to push this lot too far, Tessa joked, imagine having triplets, you would either have muscles like iron or a bad back.

When they reached the shopping parade the first shop they passed was the Charity Shop. Outside stood a Buggy. Tessa, without noticing pressed ahead with the babies. But Lisa brought up by a frugal Mother had noticed, and entered the shop. Is that buggy for sale? She asked the assistant.

Yes it only came in a few minutes ago. The girl replied. After giving it a thorough inspection, Lisa asked the price, the girl seeing Lisa's shabby clothes and shoes, named an extremely low price. More so than she would have done for a wealthier person. After all she thought, this is a Charity Shop and this poor kid certainly looked as if she needed some Charity. Lisa was delighted, for the buggy looked expensive, but she paid her money even though it took almost all she had left from her meagre savings. She proudly wheeled her new possession away, and hurried to catch up with Tessa.

Tessa heard Lisa calling to her and when she turned around she was amazed to find Lisa following her and pushing a smart buggy. Where did you get that? She exclaimed. In the Charity Shop, isn't it lovely? Lisa replied proudly. Yes it is, but I'm worried, did you make yourself bankrupt. Tessa asked. Looking concerned. No I shall be all right, and I shall get some State money next week. It would be a tight few days, but she was determined to manage and not ask for help. Although she knew that it would have been given willingly without ties.

Lisa set about cleaning and polishing her new possession. The buggy was already spotless, but Lisa was wiping it with disinfectant just for good measure. Presently Tessa came downstairs with her arms full of

Pink baby clothes and several pink blankets. Here we are she announced. All pink, just what we need, I can't use them for Jamie; Marina would be most annoyed, if I did that. In her eyes all boys have to wear blue. I've been wondering what to do about them and you've provided me with the answer. She hushed Lisa's protests, saying please take them you'll honestly be doing me a favour.

When Bart came home and heard all their news, he laughed. My goodness I'd better not cross either of you two ladies or I'll find myself in trouble. I'm sure you would never do anything bad or underhand, Lisa said loyally. If I'm ever in trouble you shall be my first Character Witness Bart said his eyes twinkling. What time were you thinking of ringing this number He asked? If we ring now Tessa said, it should be about lunchtime on the west coast. I'm only guessing that he will have gone over that side of the continent. I don't know why, it's just a feeling not a certainty. Well let's hope it's not the middle of the night where ever he is. Bart grinned. You'll certainly spoil his beauty sleep if it is.

After some discussion it was decided that Tessa should do the talking, Lisa was too nervous and Bart thought that a man's voice might put Jason off and he would not give any information. Consequently they all sat at the kitchen table, while Tessa with slightly trembling fingers rang the number that Lillian Glebe had given them. It seemed like hours although it was actually only a few minutes before the line crackled and whistled a little, and then a man's voice gave the number. Am I speaking to Jason Clarke?

Tessa asked. Who want's to know? Was the cautious reply? Oh for Goodness Sake! Tessa exclaimed. Are you Jason Clarke or not? This call is costing a fortune as it is without your playing guessing games. If you are Jason say so, and I'll put you on to Lisa, otherwise I'll cut the call and save myself a lot of money.

Tessa handed the phone to Lisa, here you speak to him, I think this might be Jason, though he wont admit it to me. Lisa took the phone and said tentatively Jason? Lisa is that really you? I was told you'd had an abortion and never wanted to speak to me again,. Nobody would give me your phone number, so I applied to be sent here to work for a couple of years. Where are you? Lisa asked Vancouver Jason replied. Look, give me your number and I'll ring you back, I don't want to lose you again. The number was given and soon the phone rang. It was Jason. Do you want us to leave you alone, Tessa whispered; Lisa shook her head, and took the phone from Tessa. She listened while Jason explained that her parents, when he had called at the house had told him that Lisa had an abortion and never wanted to here from him again. He had tried several times to find out where she was but they wouldn't tell him and he'd had to give up because he was being sent to Canada. Of course her parents weren't able to tell him where she was because they didn't know. She had left home long before.

When Lisa told Jason what had really happened he was furious and said that he would apply to return to England immediately on compassionate grounds. He was thrilled and delighted to hear that he had a baby daughter and couldn't wait to see her. Get your Birth Certificate he said, were getting married as soon as I get home. They reluctantly ended their call with many assurances of devotion to each other. Lisa was starry eyed and couldn't wait for the day when Jason would be back in England once more.

Lisa knew it would be no use asking her Mother for her birth certificate and so she applied to the records office for a copy. What a shock she had when she eventually received it. Her certificate stated. Father Unknown. She then sent for her Mothers Marriage Certificate and there was another shock for there wasn't one. Her Mother and Step Father were never married. In a daze she showed Tessa and Bart the certificates and the letter that told her that there was no record of a marriage. . Phew! Bart exclaimed. When your Mother went in for deception, she certainly didn't do things by halves did she? No wonder 'That Man' was always so horrible to me, he wasn't my father, and my mother didn't want me either Lisa sobbed., Don't cry dear, Tessa comforted her. You know that you and Jason will both make a better job of it than they did.

Once Jason arrived, everything was quickly arranged and soon it was the Wedding Day. In the short time available Tessa and Lisa had assemble a pretty wedding. Lisa looked charming in her cream outfit and Baby Angela looked as adorable as always. The problem of where to live was solved by Jason's firm. They were a large firm of builders and had recently built an estate in Hertfordshire. It was an easy train journey to London. Lisa had no wish to live anywhere near her Mother, but she was pleased to be within easy reach of Tessa, Bart and the children.

CHAPTER FIVE

While the drama had been unfolding in Hampstead. Gil and Fern had been in EastLeigh, staying at the same Beach Cottage that Gil had rented some years before, and where he had first met Fern on the beach.

Gil had hoped the familiar scenery that Fern had loved so much would help her memory, but sadly it was not so. They had taken Bitza with them, for Gil knew how fond Fern was of the little dog, and especially so because he was the only memory she had of before the accident, and she seemed to cling to him almost like a lifeline when she felt adrift and confused. Each morning they took their run on the beach. Strictly speaking it was mainly Gil and Bitza who ran, while Fern wandered slowly, now and then throwing a stick for Bitza to retrieve. She tried to be cheerful and lively for Gil's sake, but the effort drained her. Gil's heart ached for her, but he was powerless to help her much as he longed to do so. He had tried to forgive his sisters for their thoughtless action, which had caused Fern's accident. But he found it so hard that sometimes he felt as if he hated them.

One morning while Gil ran along the beach, Fern went to sit on the wooden steps that lead down to the beach. This had always been her particular place, and she threw a stick for Bitza encouraging him to fetch it to her. She heard steps behind her on the wooden boards and turned to see who it could be so early in the morning.

It was a young girl, she looked about the same age as Fern, her fair hair blew about her head like golden silk, and for an instance Fern felt as if she were looking in the mirror, although the girl was taller than her. She smiled at Fern and asked. Do you mind if I sit here too? Oh! You're Canadian. Fern exclaimed. The girl looked surprised. How did you know? She asked. I recognised your accent Fern replied. I didn't think that I had an accent, the girl said. It's very faint, but I'm a Canadian too so that's how I noticed it, Fern explained.

They sat on the steps for a while exchanging polite pleasantries., until Fern said, I'm Fern Manning from Vancouver, this is Bitza and my husband Gil is running along the beach at the moment. We're staying for a little holiday in the Cottage over there on the beach and she pointed in its direction. I'm from Vancouver too, the girl said, what a coincidence. What's your name, Fern asked? Perhaps Gil might know your family, I haven't lived there long so I don't now many folk. I'm Marcia Carlton; I'm over here backpacking. But I ran out of funds so I'm trying a job as Maid- of- all Work at a big house nearby. Presently Gil returned and Fern introduced her companion. They chatted for a while and then Marcia said that she must leave and get her Boss's breakfast. He gets very bad tempered if I'm late. She said, and hurried up the steps, calling back over her shoulder. See you again!

Gil watched her retreating form for a moment. I have a nasty feeling about that girl's situation. Why do you say that? I thought she seemed really nice. Fern said. I'm not talking about her, but about her Boss, Gil replied. He sounds a very similar type to someone very unpleasant that I used to know. If we meet her again it will be as well if we tell her where to find us if she needs a friend. I did tell her that we were staying at the Beach Cottage. Fern said. Good. I hope she remembers. Gil said, but he didn't explain why.

For several days, nothing was seen of Marcia. Then she appeared one morning skipping down the wooden steps, all smiles. Good morning she said. Fern moved over to make room for Marcia to sit beside her. You look happy today, she remarked. Marcia's smile broadened, and she held out her left hand to display a large diamond engagement ring. Congratulations Fern said, looking in amazement at the ring. It's a family Heirloom Marcia said .My fiancé says it's worth thousands. Do you think that perhaps you ought not to wear it to the beach? Fern asked with concern. Oh I guess it's insured, not to worry. Marcia replied gaily. She was still displaying its sparkling splendour when Gil returned along the beach. Marcia was engaged last night; she was just showing me her ring. Fern explained to him. Gil looked at the ring and did a double take.

Whew! That's some rock, he exclaimed. I hope it's insured? That's what Fern said, Marcia replied, but I'm not taking it off my finger if I can help it. She looked at her watch. Gee I'm late, I have to go, and running lightly up the wooden steps she disappeared. Gil watched her go with a concerned look. Thinking, I've heard those words before. I hope they're not for the same reason. He said nothing to Fern, but would be alert to anything that might happen. I just hope that particular history isn't going to repeat itself he sighed.

Fern had still not regained any of her memory, but in spite of Gil having said that she had not been happy in Eastleigh, she did actually feel more relaxed than she had been before she arrived.

In the Hospital, when she had awoken from her coma and found that she couldn't remember anyone least of all her husband, she had felt as if she were adrift in a strange place. Everyone had been so kind and caring, and yet she couldn't seem to connect with them. She felt guilty, as if she were letting everyone down, especially Gil. While she was recovering from her injuries she had been placed in the spare bedroom. Now she knew that she should change rooms and adopt the usual practice of sharing with her husband. But although kind and caring he was still a stranger to her as a person, and she couldn't relax or behave, as she knew that she should. Although she was attracted to Gil, she couldn't feel towards him as if he were her husband, there was no special spark, and she knew that there must have been before her memory loss. It made her feel guilty, although Gil never showed any signs of impatience she was sure that he must feel it. Perhaps I'll wait a while, she thought, slipping back into her comfort zone. Often she felt tearful and angry with herself. I can't even find anything in my own kitchen, she raged at herself one morning when she had been trying to bake a cake as a surprise for Gil.

She'd hunted through the cupboards and eventually located what she required. It took her twice as long to do the job, but at last she managed to make a fairly successful cake. Gil had been delighted with her surprise treat. But he was even more pleased to find Fern making was making an effort to get back to normality, for he had begun to worry about her lethargic and distant mental state. The Psychiatrist had warned him of the different stages that Fern would go through, and Gil began to feel that this was a positive move. Each week Fern seemed to improve, gradually taking on her household chores, but still she had no earlier memories and she still felt as if Gil was a stranger. This was the reason why, after a few months of impasse, Gil had decided to take Fern to England.

For several mornings there was no sign of Marcia on the beach, and then one morning just as Bitza was bringing his ball for Fern to throw once more, the sound of footsteps on the wooden steps behind her proved to be Marcia. Hullo! We haven't seen you lately, have you been extra busy? Fern greeted her. Yeah, something like that. Marcia replied, and running down to the water's edge she dived into the waves that were rolling in towards the shore. Fern frowned, that didn't seem like Marcia's usual chatty greeting. Perhaps she's tired, I'll ask her when she comes out of the water. But when Marcia did return and waded from the water, she grabbed her beach towel, wrapped it around her shoulders then swiftly disappeared up the wooden steps. What was that all about? Fern asked herself gazing after Marcia's retreating form. Gil with his long-sighted eyes had also seen what had happened, and lengthen his stride to return speedily to Fern. Is there something wrong? He asked. I don't know, Fern replied frowning. I didn't get the chance to ask her, she rushed here and as soon as she came out of the sea she rushed off again. I think something must be terribly wrong, I feel worried about her, she's so young and naïve. 'Says the old Granny,' Gil smiled. Should we go after her? Fern suggested. Perhaps we should wait until she comes to us, Gil advised. Fern wasn't convinced but she reluctantly agreed.

The next morning when Fern walked along to the steps, she found Marcia sitting on the bottom step, gazing out to sea. Fern sat down next to her saying, Hullo, not in a hurry today then? Marcia gathered her towel around her and stood up, but as she stood the towel slipped from her shoulder, revealing a huge ugly bruise that was beginning to turn into all shades of purple and blue. Fern suppressed a gasp but said calmly, have you had a fall, is that why you weren't here on the last couple of mornings. I'm clumsy and I knocked myself against the door that's all. Marcia replied as she turned to leave before Gil could reach them. Gil sat beside Fern on the steps. He was watching Bitza run in and out of the waves and occasionally threw him a stick. After a while he said. You're very quiet, what's the matter darling, are you bored. No, never that, Fern protested, but I am puzzled. Would you say that Marcia was clumsy? She doesn't appear to be. Why do you ask? Fern explained her reasons, and Gill groaned, Oh no not again. He muttered, I knew our holiday was too peaceful. He stood and offering Fern his hand he gently pulled her to her feet and draping his arm around her shoulders they walked slowly back to the cottage.

Gil had a dilemma, should he interfere or not. Marcia's situation was too similar to Fern's. His instinct was to back off and ignore his conscience.' Been there done that' he told himself, but still the doubts nagged at him. Marcia was a young teenager in a strange country; she knew and had, nobody to help her.

This situation has Bennett Dawson's hand written all over it. I thought that his spell in prison might change him. But it seems it didn't. In fact he seems to be getting worse, at least he didn't try to marry his last victim, even though she wasn't actually his sister.

Bitza was getting bored with the beach and so when Gil let him out one afternoon he trotted off to investigate a little. He hopped up the wooden steps from the beach and trotted across the lane and into the field, in the distance he could smell a house and something else, 'dogs' He entered the stable yard and sniffed eagerly for trails of any females. As luck would have it, Chloe came out of the house, she was one of a pair of breeding Afghans and she capered around Bitza yapping loudly, A man came into the yard to discover the cause of the commotion. He shouted and chased Bitza, who ran into a shed. And suddenly the door was closed and locked.

It was getting dark and Bitza had still not come back. Gil and Fern went out onto the beach calling to him. But of course there was no answer. Eventually they had to give up and wait until the morning. Fern was frantic, and would have continued to look if it hadn't been a moonless night, and pitch dark.

CHAPTER SIX

Bitza barked for a while but finding he received no attention, he sniffed around in the shed. He wasn't frightened; he had never had any cause to be frightened before. But being an inquisitive little dog he began to search around in the shed. He found some vegetables but after a few bites he abandoned these and searched for something tastier, he didn't find anything, but what he did find was a tiny hole in one corner where the wood had begun to rot. After a few sniffs, he began to dig. He was quite enjoying himself, for at home he was never allowed to dig in the garden and this was fun. It took him several hours of digging before he had made a hole large enough to squeeze through and then he was soon trotting back to the cottage.

Fern had become very distressed by the time they had given up their search for Bitza the night before. And Gil was worried that it might delay any recovery of her memory. For he set great store by the fact that Bitza was all she could remember from her pr-accident days. He was preparing to renew his search for the little dog, when a barking and scratching at the cottage door proved, when opened, to be a very grubby, tired and hungry little Bitza. Fern scooped him up and hugged him so tightly that Bitza squirmed and complained, and Gil heaved a huge sigh of relief.

While Fern was giving a reluctant Bitza a bath, Gil was trying to think where the dog could have been. I mustn't jump to conclusion he told himself, but I wouldn't be surprised if Bennett had something to do with this, it's the sort of 'sick' thing he would do. But we have Bitza safely back now, and must be more careful in future. He spared a thought for Marcia too, for he was sure that it was Bennett to whom she had become engaged, and now he was up to his old bullying tricks again. It's none of my business, he told himself, but his conscience said.' What if Bennett is getting worse and injures the girl really badly?

When Bennett had finished his prison sentence for Harassment leading to serious grievous bodily harm, he discovered that although his agent had managed his Estate adequately, he was not as particular and precise as Bennett liked. To give Bennett his due he was a good Estate Owner. He was always fair to the tenants about rents and repairs, and as long as the farmers worked their land satisfactorily he was satisfied.

His biggest over whelming fault was his vicious temper, especially to anyone who seemed weak or incompetent, and didn't do exactly as he ordered. He had realised that he was not getting any younger and he had no Heir. Who would have his Estate when he was gone? He didn't want it to be sold off for huge housing estates, and yet what could he do? The answer was that he would have to get married. And there was the problem for he never went out and socialised, in fact he seldom went anywhere unless it was to London to order a new suit or to visit his club, and he seldom did that.

Since the death of his father's housekeeper, and the subsequent moving away of his stepsister, he'd 'had a succession of housekeepers. But due to his bouts of violent temper none of them remained for very long, and he was getting desperate. When Marcia applied for the job, Bennett thought his prayers had been answered, for here was a young vulnerable girl that he could woo and train, and if successful would fulfil the roll of wife as well as housekeeper. And she would provide him with an heir. In his eyes it was the ideal solution to his dilemma.

This solution was not as easy as Bennett had anticipated, for he had never learned, the rule of 'If you want to receive you also have to give.' He knew that he would have to guard his temper or he would frighten his quarry away. At first all went well and after a few weeks of full harmony between them, Bennett decided to propose. He had one of his mother's dress rings cleaned, and booked dinner at an exclusive restaurant. All went well and his proposal was accepted.

After a few weeks the first flaw in Bennett's plan showed itself. Bennett expected Marcia to remain and act as if she were still a servant. Naturally Marcia had expected their relationship to change. But as the saying goes, 'Bennett didn't do change' and he didn't appreciate any changes to his rigid routine. He expected his breakfast to be on the table sharp at 7,30am. Lunch at 12 pm, his afternoon tea at 4pm sharp, and Dinner had to be at 7.30pm. Or he would make a great fuss about women who pretended to be housekeepers, but were incompetent. Marcia bore this constant criticism for a while, and one day she answered him back, telling him in no uncertain terms what a chauvinist he was and more. A fine old row ensued, and Bennett only just managed to stop himself from using violence. He was simmering with rage and slammed out of the house. But there was worse to come, when during one argument Bennett had pushed Marcia so violently that she fell against the doorpost bruising her shoulder so badly that she felt sure it must be broken because it was too painful to use for several days. She had been embarrassed too, because she was sure that Fern had seen the bruise on her shoulder when they had met on the beach one morning. After a second bout of violence Marcia had decided that she'd had enough and made up her mind to leave, she looked for the wallet, which contained her money and passport. It was not in her bag or anywhere in her room. She was sure that Bennett must have taken it to stop her from leaving.

Matters came to a head one evening when Bennett had been drinking and had come to her room with one thing in mind, and when Marcia had repulsed him his rage knew no bounds. He claimed that she had enticed him, and that they were engaged so what did it matter? Worst of all he grabbed her hair and tried to drag her to the bed. Marcia was terrified and fought back wildly, scratching his face with her nails Then with one mighty push he thrust her towards the bed, but Marcia missed the bed and crashed face first against the heavily carved wooden foot of the bed. She began to scream hysterically and Bennett taking fright as he done once before years ago in the same situation, he lumbered from the room and was soon snoring loudly on his own bed. Marcia gathered together her few possessions and fled. Once out of her room, she panicked, where could she go? It was past midnight, and she knew nobody in the village. Then she remembered that Fern had told her, if she ever needed any help they were staying in the Beach Cottage. Without another thought Marcia grabbed her haversack and ran downstairs, for a moment she paused at the door of the study and entering she went to Bennett's desk. By a miracle he had forgotten to lock the draw and on top of a pile of papers lay her wallet. Thankfully she took it and hurried out of the house slamming the door behind her.

Fern was asleep, but Gil was typing the last chapters of his latest book for his publisher had urged him to finish it. Bitza was dozing in his bed snuffing and whimpering, chasing his dream rabbits. Gil thought he heard a thud outside the door. Bitza jumped out of his bed and went immediately to the door., and began sniffing and whining. OK Fella I've got it! Gil exclaimed, and opening the door he looked out. For a moment he thought he had imagined the noise, and then he saw the crumpled figure on the doorstep, and a rush of 'deja vue' spread over him. There on the step lay a young girl, her long silky golden hair was spread about her like a cloak, for a moment he thought it was Fern, and it brought back a rush of tragic memories, but when he gently lifted the silken strands the battered little face revealed was not that of Fern, but of Marcia. I'll hang for that man one day, he muttered to himself as he gently lifted the girl up, and then, carrying her inside, he laid her carefully on the sofa.

Fern had by this time woken up and came to see what was causing the disturbance. When she saw Marcia's face she gasped. What's happened? Has there been an accident?

No Honey, just some Bully running true to form and showing Marcia his true nature. As he spoke he was gently dabbing Marcia's face with Arnica liniment. She groaned, and muttered. He pushed me. Yes, we know Honey, he's done it all before, and no doubt will again. You're safe now, you don't have to worry, and he'll have to go through me to get to you. I've dealt with him before, he's a bully at the best of times but when he's drunk he's worse. Gil explained.

I can't marry him now, Marcia sobbed, I should think not! Fern said fiercely, he should be prosecuted for assault. Gil didn't bother to tell them both that Bennett had not long been out of prison for exactly that crime. What shall I do about the ring? Marcia asked holding up her hand. Keep it! Gil advised her, you've earned it. But it's a family Heirloom, Marcia protested. I doubt it, Gil replied, I can't see him giving that to anyone if it were so valuable. Fern looked closer at the jewellery, actually it looks more like a dress ring, she said, and anyway I think you deserve it as compensation.

Do you have enough money to return to Canada? Gil asked. Yes Bennett paid me a very fair wage and I've saved it, so I've more than enough for the fare. Then I think that after a couple of days when you feel a little better, we should take you to the Airport and put you on a flight home. Marcia gratefully, agreed and having settled that, they were all thankful to retire to bed.

CHAPTER SEVEN

Fern had bought some picture postcards to send to Lisa, Tessa, and their families, not forgetting a special one for Marina and Jamie. They were ready to be posted and Fern decided to take Bitza with her and go to the Post Office for stamps. Strangely she seemed to know her way to the village, but perhaps it's Bitza leading me she thought, for she had put him on a lead not wanting him to run off again. When she came to the village she thought what a pretty little place it was, with its Narrow Street and old-fashioned shop fronts, there was even a real Country Pub facing the Village Green. On the pond there were some ducks. Fern sat for a while on a near by seat, which had a small metal plate, on the back. It read-.

'In memory of Miss Emily Rose Barker. 1900-2000. Our beloved School Mistress for 80 years'.

Fern sat for a while day dreaming of what the Village must have been like when Miss Emily had first begun to teach there. No cars or motor bikes, only plodding horses and trundling carts, and maybe now and then a Carriage or the Mail Post calling at the Inn. No Street lights to hide the beauty of the stars and no noisy radios or telephones. She smiled to herself and wondered how Miss Emily had coped with so many changes in her lifetime. Fern sighed and came back to reality; then rising from her seat she crossed the road to the Post Office.

It was dark inside and for a moment she didn't see Mrs Glebe. But Bitza had seen the old lady and sensing a possible biscuit or two, he jerked the lead out of Ferns unsuspecting hold and trotted round to the other side of the counter. Fern was about to recall him, when Mrs Glebe, said Hullo Bitza my lovely, have you come in for a biscuit? And she opened a small packet of biscuits,, giving a couple to the eager Bitza.Then smiling at Fern she asked. And how are you Fern Dear? I heard that you hadn't been very well, you had a nasty fall it seems. Are all your bones mended now? Yes thank you Fern replied, at a loss for what else to say. This Lady obviously knew her and Bitza too. Suddenly she remembered what she had come to get, and asked .Can I have some stamps please? Sending some Post Cards? That's nice, so many people just text now a days Mrs Glebe observed. It looked as if Mrs Glebe was ready for a Chat, and so Fern agreed that it was so, and as soon as she could without seeming too impolite she left the shop. She walked back to the Cottage, feeling rather depressed. I can't even remember the price of a stamp for a Post Card; she thought dolefully, how am I going to get on with anything more complicated?

Marcia stayed on with them for a few more days, by now her bruises had turned from purple to yellow and it was easier to cover them with makeup. The weather had been fine and the two girls and Biza were enjoying the Beach, while they left Gil in peace to finish the last of his book.

I need to go to the village and get a few toiletries. Marcia said one afternoon. Will you come with me Fern? I'm afraid that I might meet Bennett. We'll take Bitza as a bodyguard, Fern laughed. Yes, and if we do meet Bennett, we can tell Bitza to bite him. Marcia replied. Although that might not be a good idea, he might complain that Bitza is a dangerous dog and report him to the police. That's the sort of mean person he is. She added. I hope I never meet him, he sounds horrible, Fern said with a shiver, and Marcia quickly changed the subject. Shall we have tea in 'Abigail's Tea Room'? She suggested. Yes that would be lovely Fern agreed.

Their shopping completed, they entered the Tea Room, and were greeted by Abigail herself, Hello Mrs Manning, I didn't know you had come down for a holiday, where's Mr Manning? He's busy finishing his latest book, Fern replied. I look forward to reading it when it comes out, Abigail said. Now what can I get you? A pot of tea and some cake please. Marcia answered. She knew that Fern was feeling a little fazed, she had been struggling all afternoon with people that she couldn't recall who were greeting her, and that she was beginning to feel the strain. Bitza had drunk his fill at the 'doggy' water bowl and was now coping with a large dog biscuit that Abigail had given him. What about the crumbs? Fern had protested, oh, we can soon sweep them up, Abigail replied easily.

Marcia suddenly picked up one of the lunch Menu's, but she wasn't reading it, she was using it as a shield to hide behind.   What's the matter? Fern asked puzzled. It's Bennett. He stopped outside, I thought he was going to come in, but he's walked on now. Marcia replied.   He can't cause a fuss in here, Fern assured her. Abigail would call the police, if he tried to harm you. If you're worried we could ring

We could ring Gil and ask him to come and fetch us, she offered. Before their ordered tea had been served, who should come into the Tea Room but Gil? I thought I would find you ladies in here. He smiled. I'll ask Abigail to bring some more tea and cake. Fern offered, relieved to have Gil there after Marcia's sighting of Bennett.

The shop bell tinkled and Mrs Glebe came inside with a rush, excitedly waving an opened letter in her hand. I've had a letter from my Lisa she exclaimed. She's married and has a beautiful baby girl. How lovely, Fern said. That woman! Mrs.Glebe exclaimed. She tried to tell me that Lisa wasn't my real granddaughter, but I know different, because she's the image of my sister May, she's dead now, but I've got plenty of photographs. You can always find out with a DNA test. Abigail told her. How can I get that? Mrs Glebe asked. Go to your Doctor and he'll arrange it for you. Abigail replied.   I'll do that Mrs.Glebe replied. It'll give me great pleasure to prove that woman is telling lies. Everyone admired the pictures of the Wedding and the beautiful baby girl. Her name is Angela, and she looks like an Angel doesn't she? Said the proud grandma. And everyone agreed that it was true.

Mrs Grebe wasted no time in going to see her Doctor to ask about the DNA Test. She explained her reason and he was most helpful. Before long a DNA kit was in the post on it's way to Lisa. Complete with instructions. Lisa also wasted no time before sending her Sample off to the Laboratory, and waited impatiently for the result to return. When the result was revealed. Lisa couldn't believe her eyes. It was Positive. She was truly a Grebe, and her Birth Certificate was wrong. Her mother had deliberately signed that her father was unknown. Now she had discovered that George Grebe was actually her real father. Why had her mother done such a wicked thing, especially as she was not married to George. What did she have to gain? At last she decided that she would go to see her parents. Face them with the truth, and demand an explanation.

She didn't tell them that she was coming; she thought that by surprising them they would have no chance to make up excuses. Her mother was surprised to see her, and Lisa, not waiting to be invited, walked into the house where she had been so unhappy, and had thought never to visit again.

What do you want? Her mother demanded ungraciously. I've come to find out the truth. I've discovered that you've been lying to all of us for years and I want to know why? What are you talking about? Her mother blustered. I think you know what that is. Lisa replied severely. Do you know that forging a Birth Certificate is a crime? I've never forged anything. Let alone a Birth Certificate, Lillian argued. Well you forged mine didn't you? Lisa replied. Lillian remained stubbornly silent. You put' Father Unknown', when you knew that George Glebe was definitely my blood relative. Don't deny it, I've had a DNA Test and so has Grandma, and they were both proved positive. I might have known that Old Witch would be behind all this Lillian said.

She was always jealous of me because I married her precious son.

But you didn't marry him did you? You have never been married to anyone let alone my Father. Lillian remained silent, refusing to reply. Lisa waved the copies of the two Certificates in front of her. It's here in black and white. During their altercation, George Glebe had said nothing, but now he took the Certificates and after reading them returned them to Lisa. He still said nothing, for in truth he didn't know what to say. It was such a bizarre situation he could hardly believe it was true, although he knew that it was. He had no idea what to do about it. He was waiting to see what explanation Lillian would give.

After a few minutes, Lillian turned to George. You said that you didn't believe in marriage, and why did we need a piece of paper, and that you would never marry me, So I thought that if I said that I had a baby by another man you would be jealous of him and marry me, so that he couldn't marry me. But you still wouldn't marry me, and once I had signed the certificate to say 'Father Unknown' it couldn't be altered without my getting into trouble. There was a stunned silence and then both George and Lisa spoke together. Are you crazy, what sort of reasoning it that. Then Lisa offered, I could only think that you must have been suffering from acute Post Natal Depression, and that's stretching the imagination pretty far.

Lillian began to cry, I felt so Ill she explained and I hated George for letting me down .I had a bad pregnancy and a worse delivery and I ended up hating the baby too. I've been under the Doctor for years with boxes of pills for my depressions. Why didn't you tell us, Lisa demanded. I didn't think either of you would understand, and would just say I was making excuses for my bad temper. Linda was ashamed, because she knew that is exactly what they would have said. I'm so sorry Mum, Let's try again and see if we can all forgive and forget. It might be hard but it's worth a try. You'll both fall in love with my little Angela, she's such a sweetie, and I'm sure you will come to like Jason. He is a good kind reliable man and he adores his little family. If you take my advice I think it would be a great help to you both if you went to a Councillor. At least it wouldn't hurt to try and you might be surprised.

After a few moments George said, I admit that I should have told your Mother my reason for refusing to get married. It was because my parents were divorced when I was ten years old. It was a very long process and was full of bitter disputes and recriminations. I was piggy in the middle they spoke to each other through me, Tell your father this or tell your mother that, and each parent trying to convince me that it was the others fault. It was a nightmare and I dreaded each evening when the arguments raged, and I would lie in bed crying, with my head under the bedclothes trying to block out the sound of my father shouting and my mother ending in tears. At last, after what seemed like years, the Divorce was completed, my father left, and I stayed with my mother. Young as I was I vowed to myself that I would never get married, because if I were not married I would be able to just walk away from such a situation without any difficulty. Of course I have long since learned that it's not as simple as that, for even without a marriage certificate there are still emotional ties and responsibilities that bind you to the relationship. I was too proud and stubborn to admit that I was wrong. And so I have soldiered on for years, making both of us unhappy, by not willing to discuss my problem. I can see now that I should have gone to counselling years ago, but it was not the fashion in those days and since then I suppose I had got so used to being miserable, it seemed normal. I know that sounds stupid, but I you could say we have been in a rut for years, and it has taken our very sensible daughter to shake us out of it. Even if it has been done in a rather unconventional way. George said.

During his long explanation Lillian was silent, it was going to take her a while to forgive the years of heartache and uncertainty she had suffered, but she was willing to try, and perhaps going to a counsellor would help her to understand and forgive, but she thought that forgetting might be more difficult.

Lisa was satisfied with her visit, hoping that things would now improve between her parents, and she returned to Hertfordshire with high hopes that everything was going to be happily resolved,

It wasn't long before her Mother phoned and told her that she and George were at last getting married. She put the telephone receiver down and gave a great sigh. What's the matter Darling? Jason asked. Mum and Dad are getting married at last. So I won't be illegitimate any more. She replied with a huge smile.

CHAPTER EIGHT

Tessa was dusting the sitting room, and as she carefully dusted the portrait that Bart had painted of Marietta his little daughter, she saw the damaged corner of the frame, and it reminded her that it had to be sent away for repair. I wonder, she thought, if Libby's father- in- law knows anyone who would be able to restore it. Bart was upstairs working in his Studio and Tessa went up to ask him what he wanted to do about getting the frame repaired. It was decided that they would ring Libby, who had been one of her pupils and ask if her husband knew of a reliable picture framer. Libby when contacted said. As a matter of fact the picture framer will be coming to the Gallery tomorrow afternoon to collect some pictures that are to be framed for clients. If you could bring yours in before then he can take it with the others, if that suits you. Libby offered. That will be fine Bart replied. I want to come into town for some other business, so I'll see you then.

The next morning Bart took his precious, carefully wrapped, painting of Marietta, and set off for the Gallery. There were a good number of other canvasses waiting to be framed, before they were sent off to their final destinations. Bart anxiously requested that they take great care of this painting, and he had been assured that it would be perfectly safe and would be returned to him as good as new. And so he'd reluctantly parted with it and had returned home. He was still on edge about letting the portrait go, for although is had been some years since the loss of his little daughter he still thought of her, and at times wondered what she would have been like now, if she had not been killed in the motorway accident, that had almost crippled him for life. He never told Tessa of his thoughts, perhaps he should have, but she had been so good to him, first giving him the impetus to snap out of his depressions and then making a wonderful life together with a loving wife and two beautiful babies.

After two weeks when Bart hadn't heard from the Gallery about the repair of the picture frame, he became anxious and rang them to ask if it was ready. Imagine his dismay when he learned that they didn't have the painting, and could find no record of its being sent back to him.

After a frantic search by the staff at the Gallery it was discovered that the painting had been sent to Italy, together with some paintings bought by Alfredo Bellini, an Italian businessman. Bart was horrified, and said that he would go to Italy at once to recover his painting. When Signor Bellini was told, he refused to part with the paining and offered to buy it from Bart. Naturally Bart was incensed and refused, demanding the return of his property. If it had been any other one of his paintings, but not that one it was too emotionally connected to him. He had painted it to mark his daughter's third birthday, and a week after that birthday she had been killed in the accident. He had been so distressed that he couldn't even bear to have the portrait of Marietta that he had so lovingly painted anywhere in the house, and had asked Gil to hang it in the sitting room of his apartment. There it had remained until the birth of Marina, and Tessa had suggested that it would be nice to have it in their own home, so that all the family could be together, for, as she explained to Bart. Marietta is still your little girl, although she's not here in person.

In spite of Signor Bellini's refusal to part with the painting, Bart decided that he would go to Italy himself, and demand it's return, because the Gallery didn't seem to be having much success with that.

Tessa, while sympathising with Bart at the loss of his beloved painting, didn't quite understand Bart's obsession about it, for he had never opened his heart to pour out the grief that he had hidden there. He had felt that if he showed people how deeply he felt about the loss of his little girl, he would be thought of as a 'Wimp'. With the result that he had never allowed himself to grieve properly for his loss, and this unusual incident had triggered it all off, so that to others his intense concern seemed excessive.

No arguments or assurances would deter Bart and he set off for Italy prepared to do battle if necessary to retrieve his property. On arrival he went directly to the Bellini address that the Gallery had given Him. This proved to be a large Villa in Florence, with a beautiful courtyard and vine-covered canopies shading the entrance. He rang the bell, and heard it clanging in the distance. A maid answered the door and when he asked to see Signor Bellini, she showed him into a small anti room and politely asked him to wait.

Presently she returned and motioning him to follow her, she led him to a Salon where Signor Bellini awaited him.

Bart moved towards the man who rose from his chair to greet him, and then stopped in his tracks, unable to speak for his breath caught in his throat, and then he gasped. What are you doing here? I live here; I am Alfredo Bellini, and You! Are the man who killed my granddaughter. Bart couldn't believe what he was hearing, and protested. Didn't you read the results of the Inquest? It was proved to be the driver of the lorry who was at fault, he had been drinking alcohol, he claimed that it was to keep out the cold, but it was well known among his work colleagues that he was a heavy drinker, and had been warned about it several times by his Superior. He was on notice to reform or he would be dismissed.

Alfredo, shook his head, I knew nothing of this he protested. I was too upset at the time to take it all in especially as it was all written in English. I also had to cope with my daughter who was going into a decline. If my wife had been alive, perhaps it would have been different. But as you know, Marta died when Maria was a baby. When Marietta was killed and then Maria died I felt as if my family was falling apart and I was so angry that I put all the blame on to you. I'm sorry for of course it wasn't really your fault. I should have listened to you when you told me what had happened but I was too distressed. If I had done so we could have shared our grief together and comforted each other. But I hope it's not too late for us to be friends, if you can forgive me for my faulty suppositions. And he continued. When that painting was sent to me by mistake, I didn't know that it was actually Marietta, but she looked so real and exactly like her that I felt as if I could pick her up and hold her. I fell in love with the painting and couldn't bear to part with it, and so I refused to return it, and offered to buy it instead. When I was told it was not for sale, I foolishly refused to return it.

Bart noticed that the painting had been placed on the wall of the salon in a prominent position, and he felt that Alfredo wasn't being difficult but was sincere in his longing to keep the painting. He thought for a moment, and then said. Look! How would it be if I were to paint another picture of Marietta exactly the same as this one? If you will let me take this picture home, I promise I'll do that. Alfredo immediately agreed and was full of grateful expressions, which quite overwhelmed the staid English Bart. Alfredo insisted that Bart stay the night and rest before his journey home, for he could see that Bart looked tired, and Alfredo knew of Bart's' fight to regain his personal mobility.

Bart telephoned Tessa to let her know that all was well and that he would be bringing the painting home. He had also told her the amazing coincidence of Afredo being his Ex-father-in-law. He explained that Alfredo had been under a misapprehension, having thought that it was Bart who had caused the accident, which had killed Marietta, when actually it was down to the drunken lorry driver.

Bring Alfredo home with you, Tessa said impulsively. He must be lonely; he lost his granddaughter and then his daughter. No wonder the poor man felt bitterness against you when he thought it was your fault. Bart assured her that he would give Alfredo the invitation, and they would be leaving for home tomorrow.

The next morning Alfredo watched as Bart carefully wrapped the precious painting ready for his return home. Bart had thought carefully as to how he would invite

Alfredo to return home with him. He was a proud man and would not care for what he felt was pity. Finally, Bart had said. I'm rather worried about carrying this all the way to London. I wonder if you would perhaps come with me to help? You could meet my wife and the little ones. We would be delighted to have you to stay. Alfredo, at first looked doubtful, perhaps your wife will not want an unexpected guest he replied. Don't worry about that for it was Tessa's idea to invite you. Bart insisted. Very soon the two men taking the precious painting set out for the airport.

Later that day the taxi deposited the travellers in Hampstead, and very glad they were to reach their destination. Bart's Back was beginning to ache and Alfredo was feeling travel weary.

Tessa was waiting with a light meal and had the kettle on and the coffee pot ready boiling. Alfredo was welcomed and settled in to a comfortable armchair. Jamie was asleep in the carrycot, but Marina was wide-awake and very interested in the new visitor. She remained silent, observing him with her big blue eyes.

Then she came to stand before him and asked 'Are you my Grandpa?' Yes, Tessa said. This is your 'Italian Grandpa', but we will call him 'Nonno Alfredo'. Yes? She looked enquiringly at Alfredo.

Alfredo looked pleased and nodded and smiled saying. 'Si Cara,' Marina climbed trustingly on to his knee and began to tell him all about the family. Although he did not always understand what she was saying, her artless chatter enchanted him, and Alfredo felt as if he had come home.

Presently, Marina came downstairs after her bath, smelling of baby powder and ready for bed. She looked adorable in her Bunny Pyjamas. She kissed everyone, including Nono Alfredo. Will you be here in the morning Nono? She asked. At his assurance she nodded, looking pleased. I've always wanted a Grandpa, and now I 've got one, She said happily, and skipped off to bed with a last wave of her little hand.

The next morning Bart began to paint the second picture of Marietta for Alfredo. He felt it was a challenge, to see if he could repeat the picture once more and make it as realistic as he had done before. This time he was painting from memory, where as the first had been done from life. He had to admit that it had been hard work to keep Marietta still and occupied long enough to get a good likeness. This time he would be painting a still life. He worked swiftly, concentrating deeply on what he was doing, and gradually the painting began to take shape. He stood back to clean the brush he had been using and glanced critically at his work. Suddenly a strong sense of 'deja vue' came over him, and he remembered when he had reached the same point during the first painting, Marietta had jumped from the chair saying that she wanted a drink and the bathroom. He had been rather put out and had chided her. He would have given anything for that scene to be repeated now. He sighed, the mood was broken, he would come back later, and perhaps a short break would do him good.

Each day Bart worked on the painting, but he would let nobody see it before it was finished. Tessa was used to Bart and his temperament when he was working, but Alfredo thought it strange and couldn't understand why.

While Bart was closeted away in his Studio, Alfredo was enjoying being part of a happy family.

He had walked with Tessa and the children taking Marina to Nursery School. At the gate Marina had proudly announced that this was her Nonno Alfredo, from Italy, who had come to visit them. All the young mothers were delighted to meet the handsome Italian with charming manners and attractive accent. You're so lucky, they told Tessa. Our fathers-in-laws are mostly old and grumpy. Sometimes Alfredo would go alone, but not often for he was not used to so much adulation, and he felt a little overwhelmed.

One afternoon, Bart came down to the sitting room and announced. 'It's finished!' Everyone insisted on going upstairs to look. They crowded into the room and there stood the finished painting on the easel. It's still damp don't touch it! Bart warned protectively. Alfredo broke into Italian, for he did not have the words to tell Bart in English what a wonderful job he had done, and how grateful he, Alfredo was for such a priceless gift.

We must celebrate with a cup of tea, Tessa said turning towards the door. I think this deserves more that a cup of tea Bart declared. I'll open a bottle of wine. I know we don't often drink alcohol, but this is a special occasion.

Now that the painting was finished, Alfredo felt that it was time for him to return to Italy. He had a business to run and had left his manager in charge, and although they had kept in touch by phone, he felt that he must go, for there were papers to sign and other matters to settle.

Marina was very upset that her Nonno Alfredo was going away. But he promised that if he could not get back to see her again, then her Mama and Papa would bring her to Florence to see him and stay for a holiday.

When all was settled satisfactorily the precious 'new painting' was carefully wrapped and lovingly carried to Italy by Alfredo, for he would not trust anyone else to transport it. It was not as heavy to carry, as the other had been to bring home, for Alfredo intended to have it framed in Italy.

Life seemed very tame after Nonno Alfedo had gone. It wasn't long before he rang to tell them that he was safely home and all was well with his parcel.

Soon there was more excitement for Gil rang to tell them that he and Fern were coming to see them before they travelled back to Vancouver.

I'm longing to see Fern again Tessa said. If only we could find a cure for her Amnesia it would be perfect. That could take years, if ever, Bart warned her, but 'While there's life there's hope' so they say but it's not much comfort in Fern's case.

CHAPTER NINE

While so much had been going on in Hampstead, over in Vancouver Gil's two teenage sisters had been feeling very guilty about their part in Fern's accident. If only we could earn some money, we could pay for Fern to have special treatment for her loss of memory. But what could we do that would earn us a lot of money Pippa asked? Well, Molly replied, we'll have to look out for an advert for jobs.

For several weeks they scanned the papers and magazines for offers of employment. Until in one old magazine, Pippa saw an advertisement for work on a large farm in Alberta. The money looked good and food and lodgings were free. The Magazine gave a return address. Secretly they wrote off to the Magazine for further information. They kept a look out in the house Mail Box for a letter addressed to them, so that, as before, they could collect it without their parents knowing of it.

Eventually the letter came and Pippa managed to smuggle it in her pocket to read when she and Molly were alone. The letter gave instruction of where the farm was situated and how to get here.

It was now the School summer vacation, and the girls would be free for three months.

The next morning while their mother was out shopping, they packed their knapsacks with suitable clothing, made some sandwiches for the journey, and collected together all the money that they had been saving for the holidays. They left a note for their mother to say that they had taken a bus and gone to the beach for the day. Then they went out and caught a bus, not to the beach, but to the railway station.

It was a very long way to Alberta and the girls began to wish that they had not started on this adventure. But they pressed on and at last reached their destination, tired grubby and hungry.

When they left the bus that had brought them from the Railway Station, there was a long walk on the rough track, which lead up to the homestead. This didn't look to be very prosperous in their eyes, infact it looked extremely down at heel and not very welcoming. Have we come to the right place? Molly said nervously as they knocked on the shabby door. The windows were dirty and the paint was pealing from the woodwork. Shall we leave? Molly whispered. But Pippa although younger was made of sterner stuff than her sister and refused, saying, We've come this far I'm not backing out now. And she thumped loudly on the door calling. Is anyone home? There was the sound of shuffling footsteps, and an old man appeared. He frowned at them. What do you want? Coming here, and making a racket. He complained. We've come about the jobs you advertised in the farm magazine. What jobs, I've never heard of any jobs. He grumbled. But you advertised them Pippa protested. It said 'Farm work with good wages, bed and board included'. That wasn't me, must have been my son Ed. He thought I needed help so he put an Ad in the Farmers Magazine. He's not here now, he left long ago, said he'd go and try his luck in the city. Now he's a War Correspondent, and I never know where he is. He usually sends me money each month, but I haven't heard from him lately. But we've come all the way from Vancouver, Pippa protested. What are we going to do now? We've spent our money on the fares and were hoping to earn some from this holiday job to help our sister get better from her illness, as well as our fare home. The old man scratched his head. I don't know what you can do, but there's no job here, well not for money anyway, but plenty you can do for nothing.

The girls were dismayed, and Molly began to cry, no need to be crying Little Maid, the old man said kindly, you can sleep in the bunkhouse; we got no one else working here so we don't need it. I got some Hominy grits on the stove and you can come in and eat with me if you're hungry. Realising that there was nothing that they could do about their situation at the moment, the girls took their bags to the Bunk house and returned to the Homestead, where the old man was in the kitchen pouring out three dishes of what looked like porridge, but proved to be rice. It looked very unappetising to the girls, but surprisingly when milk and honey were added I tasted passable, especially as they were very hungry, for their sandwiches had been eaten long ago.

Molly took their dishes to the sink; it was full of used cups and dishes. She 'Tutted' to herself and set about restoring order to that, and the rest of the kitchen. Once that had been done to her satisfaction she turned her attention to the Bunk House. If we have to sleep in there I don't want any mice or spiders for company, come on Pippa you can help clear up, you'll be sleeping there too don't forget.

The Bunk House was surprising tidy, and not too dusty. They swept the floor and Molly hung two bedrolls outside in the fresh air. The accommodation didn't have much in the way of comfort but did have a chemical toilet and an electric shower. Pippa pulled a face Yuk! What a dump. She complained. It could be worse, there could be nothing at all Molly chided her. Molly began hanging up their clothes, while Pippa was looking around outside. In a shed among some garden tools she found an old byecycle. It was old fashioned but seemed in good order; She took it outside and began to ride it around the yard.

Presently Molly came to look for her. Oh there you are! She said. What are you doing with that Cycle?

I'm testing it out, Pippa replied. I've been thinking, that since we have no money and there is no job here, perhaps we could just stay here for a while, and I could go into town and get a job in a Diner or Soda Bar. I've done it before. If so, this cycle would be ideal for me to use as transport. What do you think? I think that before you start making plans we should go in and ask if it's convenient for us to stay here.

When the girls returned to the house, they found the old man making a pot of tea. Suddenly they remembered their manners and introduced themselves properly. I'm Phillipa Manning and this is my sister Mary. But we're usually called Pippa and Molly, and are you Mr.Abe Grant? Pippa asked, for her sharp eyes had noticed a letter with that name, tucked beside the clock on the mantle shelf. Abe assured them that he was Abe Grant. And what are you two youngsters doing, travelling alone so far from home? Abe asked them. We wanted to earn some money to help our Sister-in-law get better from her memory loss. Pippa, always the chatterbox, then preceded to tell Abe about their winning the Ski Weekend. And the disaster that had followed. Abe listened gravely tutting now and then and shaking his head in wonderment.

My, my, you sure know how to worry your folks don't you? And now you've come away, telling them that you were going to the Beach. But instead you've come here, hundreds of miles from your home. They must be frantic with worry and I'm sure that by now they've called the police, who are no doubt looking for you at this moment.

The girls looked anxiously at Abe. Do you really think the police are looking for us? They asked.

If I were a betting man I would put money on it. Abe replied. I think you should phone your Pa and Ma right away and let them know that you're safe. He took the phone from the dresser and set it on the table for them.

After some discussion it was decided that Molly should make the call. When she at last got the connection and heard her mother's voice, she bust into tears. Pippa grabbed the phone from her sister and said. It's OK Mom we're safe. After the explanations and recriminations and when calm had been restored, her mother said. Your Dad will be up immediately to collect you both. No Mom, we don't want to be collected, we want to stay here and help Abe. He's alone and has nobody to help him. He has arthritis, he can't even cycle into town, and has to rely on whatever help he can get, and that's not much. Will you speak to my Mom? She asked Abe, handing him the phone. After a long conversation with Abe, and assurances from him that the girls could safely stay with him, Abe gave Dora Manning the telephone number of the local Padre, so that she could reassure herself that the girls were truly safe, and would have at least one responsible person to keep an eye on them.

Molly was up early, but even so Abe had been up before her, for the stove was burning brightly and a pile of newly chopped wood lay in the basket beside it. . The kettle was singing and a black and white cat was curled up in the hearth. Molly began to set out the cutlery, blue bowls, and plates, which she had discovered in the cupboard beside the chimneybreast. She had the teapot ready and was about to look for the tea caddy, when Abe came through the back door. You're up early Little Maid, he greeted her, couldn't you sleep? Yes, but I thought I would get breakfast ready. I'll go to the store later and get some groceries. No need, Abe replied, there's food a plenty here, far more that I need. Some of the ladies from the church come and stock my cupboards now and again. They're very good to me since my wife passed away.

Presently Pippa came in yawning and stretching, did you sleep well then? Abe asked. Yes like a log, Pippa replied. We tried to sleep on the train when we were coming here, but it wasn't easy. Is it OK if I use the cycle in the shed to ride into town? She asked. I wanted to try and get a job serving in the Diner; I noticed one when we were waiting for the bus. Sure you can, Abe said. It's heavy and slow but it'll get you there. If you try for a job at the Diner, tell Dolly Porter that you're staying with me and I sent you. You'll know who she is. She's a 'Big Gal with Yeller hair'. Don't think its natural like, but she's a good sort inspite of her looks. Breakfast over, Pippa set off on her journey. She found the old cycle heavy going, for it was slow and cumbersome, but Pippa thought. It must be as good as going to the gym and it's free.

She found the Diner easily, for it was close to the Bus stop and had several trucks and motorbikes parked outside. A loud bell tinkled as she entered and several diners looked up to see who was entering. One boy especially noticed her; it was the town Lothario, Lenny Small. He was lounging against the counter when she went to give her order and speak to the Owner. He leered at Pippa and drawled, 'Hi Doll! Come and sit with me, and you never know I might buy you a Soda if your good enough. What a 'Sleeze Bag' Pippa thought giving him a cold stare. No thank you, she replied. I've come to speak to Mrs Porter. At that moment Dolly Porter came through the swing door from the kitchen carrying three plates of food, these she thrust into Pippa's arms saying hurriedly, 'These are for number seven'. Pippa narrowly missed dropping the plates, but just managed to balance them equally and turned to find number seven, Luckily the tables had numbers printed on them and Pippa was able to serve them without any mishap. Pippa returned to the counter, but to her consternation the same scenario was repeated several more times. Wow! Pippa thought. They must be

Short handed here, when they need a passer by to serve at the tables.

CHAPTER TEN

Eventually the plates stopped coming and Pippa waited for Dolly to appear behind the counter. She hadn't long to wait, for soon Dolly came from the kitchen saying, Haven't you cleared the empty tables yet? I'm sorry, Pippa replied, but I'm not the waitress here, although I have come to ask you if there's a job vacancy. Dolly gave a start of surprise,

'Oh my stars' she exclaimed, I'm so sorry Honey. I thought you were the new girl who was supposed to start today, but I guess she bombed out on me. What can I get you; it's on the house by way of apology. What I would really like is a job. Pippa explained. Abe Grant sent me to you. My sister and I are staying there during the Vacation, and I want to pay for our keep.

Dolly Porter, looked at the young girl, and could see that she was from a good home and knew how to be polite and more importantly she seemed to be good in an emergency, and there were plenty of those in a busy Diner. She was extremely pretty, but She had not responded to Lenny Small and his smart mouth. She's just the girl I'm looking for and she comes with Abe's recommend, I can't go wrong. Come with me, she invited, what's your name gal. Pippa Manning, Pippa replied.

In the kitchen Pippa was fitted out with a dark mauve apron and cap with the logo 'Dolly's Diner' blazoned across it in bright yellow. Dolly explained the procedure of serving and collecting plates, which had to be swift when they were busy, don't want to get the name for being slow servers, or they'll go some place else. Dolly explained. You'll be OK in an emergency I can tell, she assured Pippa, and secretly Pippa hoped that Dolly was right.

The breakfast rush was over and Pippa was wiping down the tables ready for the lunchtime crowd. Do you have busy lunch times? She asked Dolly. Yeah, mostly we do, Dolly replied, but you'll be OK just keep going and don't stop to talk, and don't drop anybody's dinner in their lap. She laughed at the expression on Pippa's face. I had a girl like that one time, a proper klutz she was and no mistake. But you'll be OK; you managed this morning didn't you? Pippa felt more confident now. Have you ever done a job like this before? Dolly asked. Yes for a while, Pippa replied, until my Mom found out. I was only twelve years old and tall for my age so I lied, I really wanted that Job to buy a puppy. Dolly laughed, and did you get the Puppy? Dolly asked. Sadly no, Pippa said. We already had a dog and a cat and Mom thought that was enough.

The day passed quickly and although they were busy Pippa enjoyed the jokes and pleasantries from the customers. Much to her relief she saw no more of Lenny Small. Dolly had warned her against him, but she needed no warning for the little she had seen of him she didn't like or trust

Cycling back to the farm that evening Pippa felt tired, but pleased with her first day at the Diner, she had not mixed up any of the orders or dropped somebody's dinner in their lap. She smiled, thinking what a commotion that would have caused, and Dolly certainly wouldn't have said. See you tomorrow Honey, you did 'Good' today.

Molly had been busy all day too, for she had found some tins of paint in the shed, and had decided to give the front door a new coat of paint. She found the necessary tools also in the shed. When she had been a Girl Scout, for one of her badges she had to do some charity work and she chose to help old people who had no family living near. One old man, Bill Dobbs, had shown her how to do decorating on walls and woodwork. It might come in handy one day Gal when you get older and have a home of your own. You were right Bill, she thought It has come in handy, but not for that reason.

When Pippa arrived back at the farm, she didn't recognise the smart new appearance, and congratulated Molly on her hard work. Molly in turn wanted to hear about Pippa's Day. She didn't like the sound of Lenny

Small. He sounds like a real Creep, best to stay away from him she warned. Don't worry I intend too Pippa replied. Dolly had given Pippa a large plastic box of food to bring home, for as she had explained. No body will want it tomorrow and it will only be wasted, so you might as well take it for Abe and both you girls.

The days ran happily on, even the weather was ideal, the girls were beginning to feel glad that they had come, for Abe was a dear old chap, and so grateful for the chores that they did for him. All was going well until one morning as Pippa cycled to the Diner, she met Lenny Small on the road. He was driving too fast in an old pick-up truck. He deliberately revved up as he passed Pippa on the dusty road, and smothered her with dust and small stones. He drove on laughing and jeering, leaving Poppa behind him, coughing and choking.

When she arrived at the Diner, Dolly looked at her in amazement, saying' My Stars" what happened to you, have you been in an accident Gal? Lenny Small happened to me that's what. Pippa replied as she stripped off her T-Shirt and went to shake it out of the back door. You need to keep away from that 'No good trouble maker' Dolly warned her. Yes so everyone keeps telling me, but will he keep away from me, that's the problem. Every chance he gets he goes out of his way to annoy me, I wish he'd find somebody else to pester. Trouble is you're too pretty Gal. But I'll have a word with him, not that it will do much good mind, but it's worth a try.

One evening when Pippa was cycling home, Lenny drove along beside her in his truck. Wanna come out with me tonight Doll, he shouted above the engine noise. Pippa shook her head; she had no breath to speak, for she was cycling too hard to get away from Lenny. But he continued to drive alongside her, covering her with dust. At last she reached the Homestead and rode into the yard, not till then did Lenny turn the truck around and drive away laughing loudly. I think that boy must be unbalanced Pippa thought it's not normal to behave like that. Abe happened to be in the kitchen when Pippa came in. When he saw Pippa's dishevelled state, he said anxiously, have you had an accident Little Maid? Pippa shook her head.

No Abe, it's that wretched Lenny Small. He won't leave me alone. I refused to go out with him, and so he keeps pestering me. Abe was concerned. Look at the state of you he frowned? How long has this been going on? He demanded. Ever since my first day at the Diner, Pippa replied. Then it's time it was stopped, Abe said grimly. And he lifted the phone and began to dial.

CHAPTER ELEVEN

Is that the Juvenile Department? It's. Abe Grant here, I want to report one of your delinquents who's harassing one of the young friends I have staying here. She is only a schoolgirl and he's a youth of nineteen and should know better. Millie Stuart the Youth Liaison Officer sighed. What has Lenny Small done now? Mr Grant. He's deliberately intimidating a sixteen-year-old schoolgirl, because she is rejecting his very dubious friendship. In other words he's stalking her. If I were younger I wouldn't be bothering you with this problem, I would do what we always did with young teenagers when they stepped out of line. They wouldn't want a second dose. But unfortunately now it's all Namby Pamnby we must understand them and their hormones. Leave it with me, Millie said wearily; I'll deal with it. After she had rung off she said to herself. Sometimes I wish that we could deal with this in the old fashioned way, it would be so much easier. But unfortunately, knocking one devil out usually knocks another one in. and you end up with a violent adult.

Pippa neither heard nor saw anything of Lenny for several days, and then one morning he entered the Diner. He looked as if he had the remains of a black eye, and Dolly said. Well, Lenny, you've been fighting again I see. Something like that he growled, and slumping into an empty Booth, he sat glaring morosely towards the counter. Are you ordering or just taking up space, Dolly asked tartly. If you're not ordering what is it you're here for. I'm waiting. He growled. Well wait outside, Dolly ordered. Your scowl's enough to put off the customers. Lenny grunted something rude under his breath and left. But he didn't go far, for he had a grudge to pay off and he was determined to do it.

When Pippa had finished her shift, she gave a relieved sighed as she changed her shoes, for although she enjoyed her job, she did find it very tiring and could feel sympathy for some girls who were not so fortunate as her and this would be their job for life. She left the Diner by the kitchen door where her cycle was propped against the wall, but what a shock she had when she saw it, for the tyres were shredded to ribbons. There was no possible chance that she could ride it home. Pippa went back into the Diner, What's the matter Honey? Dolly asked when she saw Pippa's woe begone face. Pippa, trying to swallow her tears, replied. Somebody has shredded my tires. That Lenny Small will be the culprit I'll be bound Dolly exclaimed. He was in here earlier with a black eye and a face like a wet week. It must be his revenge for Abe reporting him to the Juvenile Officer. Pippa said. But how can I get back to the farm now? Don't worry Honey, My nephew Nate is staying with me for his Summer Vacation from University, he'll be glad to take you back in his Run About.

Nate Stevens proved to be a cheerful good-looking lad with brown curly hair and laughing brown eyes. He was sympathetic about Pippa's cycle tires and offered to repair the cycle for her. It's not actually my cycle, Pippa explained, but I shall need to get it repaired because I have no other way to get to the Diner in the mornings. Nate swung the cycle up on to the roof of his car and secured it. Right! We're ready to go, he declared. In no time at all they were drawing up in front of the Farm House. He went in to the house with Pippa to make himself known to Abe. It seemed to the girls a natural thing to do, for Abe had become like the grandfather that they had never had.

Abe was pleased when Nate offered to repair the cycle and chatted to him, subtly gaining information about the young man, for he felt protective of the two girls, since they had decided to stay and help him. Presently, Nate said that he must go and help his aunt clean up at the Diner, ready for the morning. I'll call for you at Seven am. He told Pippa, if that's OK? Then he drove away with a wave of his hand from the car window. Well he's a bit of a' dreamboat, isn't he? Molly remarked as the taillights of

Nate's car disappeared down the road. Pippa didn't answer, her feelings were too private to be shared lightly.

In the morning Pippa was ready and waiting when Nate arrived, bringing with him the repaired cycle. How much do I owe you? Pippa asked him. Dolly paid for the tyres, Nate replied. She said that as the cycle was left outside her back door she would be responsible for its repair. But it wasn't Dolly's fault, Pippa protested.

Take my advice, never argue with Dolly, she always wins, it's well known in the family, and Nate grinned.

But she did say that it would be best to keep the cycle in the storeroom next to the kitchen, just to keep it safe from any more sabotage.

Each morning Pippa cycled to the Diner and each evening Nate would put her cycle on top of his little car and drive her home. It is kind of you Nate, Pippa said. But you don't need to go out of your way, I expect Dolly would prefer you to stay and help her clear up in the Diner. Actually Dolly suggested that I drive you home, Nate replied. I think she's worried that Lenny Small might start his nonsense again. I haven't seen him at all lately, Pippa said. Maybe not, Nate answered. But that doesn't mean he's not planning something. He was pretty mad at Abe for reporting him to the Juvenile Officer. He's the sort that bears a long grudge and is willing to wait to get his own back.

Nate had returned to the Diner after taking Pippa back to the farm after her shift, and he began to take the clean dishes from the Dishwasher, and stack them in the cupboard. Dolly was making a list of the provisions she needed to stock up the freezer. Did you get Pippa home OK? She asked casually. Sure, as always, Nate replied. She's tall for a girl of sixteen, isn't she? Dolly asked once again. What are you trying to tell me Dolly? If it's a warning, Nate said, I already know that she's a minor, if that's what worrying you. But she'll grow up, and I have my own agenda on that. Fine, just so you know that's all. Dolly replied with a sigh of relief, and no more was said on the subject. But, unknown to Dolly or Nate, Pippa had her own thoughts on Nate, but she was keeping her hopes and dreams to herself.

Lenny Small's anger against Abe for reporting him to the Juvenile Officer was still simmering, and he spent some time thinking of how he could pay him back and also that snooty mare Pippa. What a stupid name, just as stupid as her he thought immaturely. He wasn't bright enough to realise that it was just a shortening for the name Phillipa.

Nate's car had a puncture; he had taken it to the garage, but Hank Mills was busy at the garage. Todd Ford, his mechanic was off sick with two broken arms, from a motorcycle accident. The result of the fact that he liked to drive at a reckless speed, but even though there was very little traffic on the roads, he had managed to crash into a second reckless driver who turned out to be Lenny Small. His bike had skidded across the road on its side with Todd underneath it, and he was lucky to be alive.

A new tire had to be ordered for Nate's car and reluctantly Nate realised that Pippa would have to ride her cycle home for he would be unable to take her in the car.

Pippa set off on the cycle, after many instructions from Nate about being wary of anyone offering to give her a lift. He was thinking of Lenny, but he didn't want to alarm her. Pippa was half way home when she heard the sound of a vehicle being driven at speed coming up behind her; she drew to the side of the road to let them pass. But the truck skidded to a halt in front of her, it blocked her path, her cycle wobbled, and she fell off. She began to struggle to her feet saying furiously. Don't you ever look where you're going? You're not the only one on the road you know. Then to her consternation she saw that it was Lenny Small. Oh no! I might have known it would be you! She exclaimed. Just the sort of behaviour I would have expected from a lunatic like you., What's the matter with you are you blind or just plain stupid?

Who're you calling Stupid? Lenny shouted, you were in the middle of the road. And you were driving too fast.

Pippa replied angrily. For in truth she had been badly frightened, especially as she was still some way from the farm, and she didn't know what Lenny would be up to next, he looked wild eyed as if he had been drinking alcohol or something bad. Pippa took a deep breath trying to calm her self. She picked up the cycle and prepared to mount, intending to ride home. But Lenny had other ideas. You're coming with me, he said, advancing towards Pippa with the intention of grabbing her and dragging her into the truck.

To his surprise, Pippa didn't scream and run as he had expected, she waited calmly until he came within easy reach, then suddenly she acted, and Lenny didn't know what happened, but he found himself lying on the floor in a Lock Hold with Pippa kneeling on his back. He couldn't move he was so dazed by her sudden attack.. Now listen to me Lenny Small, Pippa said. I'm only going to tell you this once. If you ever try anymore of you lousy tricks on me again, next time I'll dislocate your shoulder or worse and don't think I couldn't, because I took my certificates in Self Defence and I passed with honours. I shall be reporting you to the Miss Stuart at the Youth Liaison Office, and if I have any more trouble from you I'll tell the police. You've been drinking Alcohol, and I'm sure they wouldn't be pleased to hear that. I don't want to get nasty with you, but your getting on my nerves, so back off and leave me alone. Is that clear? She asked giving Lenny a slight shake. He mumbled what she hoped was a 'Yes', and she released him. Then mounting her cycle she continued her journey home. Her knees were shaking and she listened anxiously hoping that Lenny wouldn't decide to follow in the truck and run her down. She reached the farm without further mishap, but she was shaking when she dismounted from the cycle and leaned against the wall for a moment to collect herself and just at that moment Abe came out of the door and saw her.

What is it Little Maid are you ill? He asked in alarm. No, Abe! It's OK, I'm just a little shaken. Why! You're trembling like a leaf Abe said in concern, come inside and sit down. He gave her something in a glass that stung her throat, she didn't know what it was but it stopped the trembling.

For the first time Abe noticed her dishevelled appearance. Did you have an accident on the road? He asked her. Not exactly. Pippa replied. She was reluctant to tell Abe what had actually happened for she knew that he would be furious with Lenny, and would immediately phone the police. What do you mean not exactly, looks to me as if you've been in some sort of trouble, look at the state of you, and your clothes are torn too. If I tell you, will you promise not to be cross? Pippa asked anxiously. I won't make false promises, but I will listen, although I know I'm not going to like what I hear, because I have a shrewd suspicion that this involves Lenny Small. Abe replied grimly. When Pippa had told her tale, Abe said. Right! That boy has gone too far, I'm reporting him to the police. But I promised him that I wouldn't do that if he behaved himself. Pippa protested.

You might have promised Abe replied, but I didn't. There's something very wrong with that boy, and he needs special help. He's been in trouble for years, but now he's getting worse, he's unpredictable, and I've a suspician that he's drinking hard spirits too. Though where he gets the money who knows, for he doesn't have a job. He's so unreliable that nobody will employ him..

At that moment Molly came in to the kitchen and when she saw the state of Pippa she was shocked. Have you had an accident? She asked. I had an argument with Lenny Small. Pippa replied with a grin, She was feeling better now and could see the rather twisted comical view of the affair. But when she told Molly what had happened her sister didn't see anything amusing about the situation. That boy needs locking up she declared. When later Nate called in to see if Pippa had arrived home safely he was horrified to learn what had happened, and blamed himself for letting her go home alone. It wasn't your fault your car had a puncture, Pippa comforted him, but it was lucky I had those classes in self defence. I wasn't going to go to the Self Defence Class, but the Class I wanted, which was Yoga, was full, and I went to the Self Defence Class instead.

I'm glad that I did that Class now, for as a consequence of that; I was able to give Lenny the shock of his life, when a girl half his size knocked him down and locked him in a death grip. Well not quite death, she laughed, but very uncomfortable any way. How can you laugh about it, Molly exclaimed, you could have been seriously hurt or anything horrible could have happened if he had dragged you into his truck.

If he'd done that. Nate declared, he would have been very sorry I could tell you. If I had got hold of him, never mind GBH and Assault and Battery, It would have been more like Murder.

Nothing was seen of Lenny for a while, and it was a relief to Pippa, for she had begun to dread being accosted by him again. Millie Stuart came into the Diner one morning asking for Pippa, who was in the kitchen filling the dishwasher. Dolly called her and Pippa came to see what she wanted. Millie had come in to tell them that Lenny had been sent away to a Remedial Centre. Where he would have Psychiatric Therapy to help him to lead a normal life. His Childhood had been unspeakably bad and he had grown up believing that way of life was normal. Apparently he had settled down well and was making progress and Millie said they had high hopes of his turning into a decent citizen before too long.

CHAPTER TWELVE

The summer was gradually drawing to a close. The blackberries were ripening and other fruits were heavy on the trees. Do you make jam? Molly asked Abe one morning. No Little Maid, not anymore. That was my Ginny's department when she was alive, a rare dab hand she was with the Jam and bottling the fruit, plus freezing the vegetables. I don't have any call for such things now. Would you mind if I made some Jam? Molly asked. If you want to try, it's all right by me, Abe replied. Just don't burn the house down, he joked. For the next few days Molly was busy picking, washing and cooking the fruit until at last she had several rows of jams and preserved fruit, proudly displayed on the dresser.

The next morning, Nate arrived to take them all to church. They all enjoyed going each week, It was a bright cheerful service and everyone gathered afterwards for tea or coffee. News was exchanged, and babies admired, before they went home to prepare their Sunday lunch.

While they were out a Taxi drew up in front of the house, and a tall man stepped out. He paid the driver and turned towards the front door. This as usual was not locked. Entering the kitchen he looking around and gave a sigh of relief. Then he went upstairs and throwing off his jacket and bag, he dropped down onto the bed and fell asleep.

Presently Abe and the girls returned, and Molly began to prepare the lunch. While Abe put more wood on the stove and Pippa went out to feed the hens and look to see if there were any eggs in the nesting boxes. Molly went upstairs to put some freshly ironed clothes away. Suddenly Abe and Pippa heard Molly's scream, and she came running down the stairs., shaking with shock

There's a man in Abe's bed she cried. For a moment there was silence, and then both Abe and Pippa made a rush for the stairs

Pippa reached the bedroom first and always a practical girl she approached the bed cautiously, but the occupant lay prone and seemingly unconscious or dead. But Pippa immediately looked for a pulse and finding it was beating strongly, she shook the man's shoulder. Molly hovered at the door, but Abe who had been looking closely at the man, suddenly exclaimed, He's my son, Ed! And he too shook the man's shoulder, saying urgently. Wake up Ed. It's me, Pa!

Ed Grant opened his eyes to find three pairs of eyes gazing down at him. His father's, and one pair bright blue and alert the other soft brown and looking sympathetic. He struggled to a sitting position, and extended his left hand, saying wryly, Ed Trent. Ex -War correspondent. Then turning to Abe he said. Hullo Pa. As you can see the bad penny had returned. Abe took his hand and leaning forward hugged him. Welcome Home son, he murmured through his tears.

Ed rose with difficulty from the bed and followed the other three downstairs. Are you hungry? Molly asked solicitously, putting on the kettle. No thanks, but I would like a cup of tea. I haven't had a decent cup of tea for years. He smiled a kilowatt smile at her and she smiled shyly, turning away to take the cups from the cupboard.

Seated at the table with their tea. Abe noticed that his son, who usually, used his left hand. Was now using his right hand. What's wrong with your hand Son? He asked bluntly. Oh, I just had a bit of a 'Prang' in a car that's all, Ed said dismissively. Looks more than that to me his father insisted. You might as well tell me now; I'm bound to find out everything in the end.

You always were a nosey old so and so, weren't you Pa? Ed laughed. As a matter of fact I've been in hospital for some time. That's why you haven't heard from me. I was in an armoured car following and reporting a skirmish in Afghanistan when we ran over a mine, The driver was killed and I was thrown out at a distance, which was lucky for me because the enemy thought I was dead, they were on the run and didn't bother to check, otherwise they would have shot me. They took no prisoners, it was too inconvenient, unless they were likely to have information, which they knew we didn't.

Why didn't the authorities inform me of this? Abe demanded. They didn't know who I was, because I wasn't in the Press car, but had hitched a ride with one of the lads. In other words I wasn't supposed to be there. My camera bag and identification were all blown to bits and it was too dangerous for anyone to go and search for fragments, which probably didn't exist any more. I was unconscious for a while, and when I eventually did come round I couldn't remember a thing. Not my name or the reason for my being there. I was wearing a uniform that I had borrowed, because my own clothes were covered in blood when I was helping to rescue some of the other chaps who had been caught in an ambush. The only solution was to send me to Hospital to be patched up.

I've been in the Military Hospital ever since. I can walk now, and my memory has returned, although I'm still not good at remembering birthdays, He joked. What about your right hand? Abe asked. Trust you to notice Pa; I could never get away with anything your eagle eye always noticed what I was up to. But seriously Pa, it's not too bad, and I'm still having Physio for that.

Pippa, who planned to train as a nurse when she left school, was full of interest and asked Ed many questions about the type of treatment he had received. While Ed was answering Pippa's questions. Molly had gone upstairs to make up the second bed. She placed the expensive jacket on a hanger and placed his bag on the bed. Returning to the kitchen she found that Pippa was still questioning Ed. Molly, looking at his tired face and drooping figure intervened. I think that's enough questions for now Pippa, let Ed have a rest. No doubt he's been travelling for a long while to get here and would like to continue the sleep that we so rudely interrupted.

Ed rose from his chair and placing his cup on the table, he smiled at Molly saying. Yes 'Ma'am'. I bow to you orders; He then took himself off to bed to dream of a gentle girl with a soft voice, a sweet smile and dreamy brown eyes.

Ed woke late the next morning. He could hear someone with a musical voice singing along to the radio. Rising and going to the bathroom, he was soon washed and shaved and going down to the kitchen where he found Molly, busy with the household chores. She looked up and smiled at him as he entered. 'Cup of tea?' She offered, putting the kettle on the stove. 'Great idea' Ed replied. I like this Hotel, it's the best service I've ever had. He joked. Well don't get too used to it, Pippa and I will be going home before too long, I have to go to UNI and Pippa has to finish High School if she wants to be a nurse. It's a long time since I was at UNI, Ed replied. So says the 'Old Grandpa' Molly laughed. At the moment I feel like one, he said ruefully.

What do you plan to do while you are here convalescing? Molly asked. What I had planed to do once I gave up the 'War Zones' reporting was to come home and run the farm with Pa for a while, but it seems I'm too late. He has now rented out all the land to a neighbouring farmer, and just kept the house and garden.

Don't give up, you can still write though can't you? Molly encouraged him. You must have so much to tell of your experiences, and can tell the world of the brave troops who were wounded or killed. They gave their lives to help a terrorised people. The world should hear how brave they were, and what they had to contend with. You could make it your personal project as a memorial to those who never returned. And it's quiet and peaceful here so that you can concentrate easily. Apart from which you look as if you need some peace and quiet yourself and some TLC from your family.

Ed was touched by her kindness, and thought to himself, I've never met a girl like her; she is the girl for me, if she were older I'd ask her out, but she wouldn't want an old crock like me. Little did he know that Molly was wishing that he would ask her out for she felt a strong empathy with him. Is it because he's been ill and I feel that he needs somebody to love and care for him? She asked herself? But she knew that was not the reason, it was a deeper feeling and one she had never felt before. And young as she was she knew that her instinct was right. I guess I shall have to wait and see what happens, for I'll be going back home soon, and maybe if he asks for my address perhaps he'll keep in touch.

Unknown to Molly, Pippa too was feeling reluctant to leave, because she would miss Nate. She knew that he thought of her as a schoolgirl. But she would grow up one day, and perhaps he would then return her feelings. If he doesn't find somebody else before then, she thought gloomily. But like Ed's feelings for Molly, Nate too had made up his mind that Pippa was the girl for him, and was longing for the day when she was old enough for him to tell her how he felt. He did manage to drop a hint by saying that because he was training to be a doctor; he would have to marry a nurse. Pippa hoped that he was talking about her, but she didn't have the courage to ask.

The last few days at the farm seemed to fly past and soon it was time to pack their bags. Nate drove them to the bus station Pippa sat in front with Nate and Molly and Ed in the back seat. Much to the girl's relief, they had all exchanged addresses and phone numbers. When the bus arrived both the girls said goodbye to the boys and with a last goodbye hug and a kiss, they boarded the bus and waved from the window until they were out of sight. At the train station they boarded the train for Vancouver. Neither of them said much, they were feeling too miserable at the parting from the two men, but at least had the comfort of knowing that they had the addresses and phone numbers of both of them.

It was a long tiring journey on the train. They tried to sleep, but neither of them managed more than a few minutes at a time. Then at last they were drawing in at their home station, and they tumbled out of the train travel worn and weary. How relieved they were to be met by the smiling faces and hugs of their parents. The recriminations and questions would come later, but they were home. Although neither of them had earned the required money to pay for any treatment for Fern.

They dutifully telephoned Abe to let him know that they were safely home, and to thank him once again for his Hospitality in spite of their having arrived at his home uninvited.

The Summer Vacation was over, on the whole it had been a good experience, and both girls returned to their Studies, both still dreaming of Ed and Nate, and hoping that it would not be too long before they heard from both of them.

CHAPTER THIRTEEN

In England it had been an unusually good summer, with long warm sunny days and Fern and Gil had decided to stay on at the cottage. Gil had reached a critical part in the latest book that he was writing, and so Fern and Marcia spent long hours on the beach or walking with Bitza in the early mornings and evenings. . On one of these walks they had seen Bennett in the distance with Chloe, and had only just managed to catch hold of Bitza before he took off after the beautiful Borzoi bitch. Phew! That sure was a close shave, Marcia exclaimed as Fern managed to clip the lead onto Bitza's collar. I wish Bennett would keep Chloe in the house and not let her run free when she's on heat. Marcia grumbled. But when did Bennett ever do anything sensible or considerate?

I have to go up to Town to see my publisher. Gil announced one morning. Would you girls like to come, we could stay for a few days, show Marcia the sights and take in a few Shows. What do you think? I think it would be great! Marcia declared. What about you Fern, do you feel up to it? Gil asked. Yes that would be a good way for me to see places that I know but can't remember. Fern replied. And so the next day they locked up the cottage and taking Bitza with them they set off for London.

Fern couldn't believe that she had lived and travelled about in this great busy place, every thing and everyone seemed to be in a rush. But after a few days she became used to the bustle and began to enjoy visiting the places of interest, and the Theatres, with Shows from Musicals to Shakespeare. She didn't however enjoy the stomach wrenching lift rides up and down to Gils High Rise apartment.

In Gil's apartment, Mrs Miller, his Housekeeper, was pleased to see Fern again and sympathetic about her memory loss. Marcia was intrigued by the view of London that could be seen from Gils Balcony and wanted Gil to name all the buildings that they could see. A task somewhat beyond him, but Mrs Miller was able to oblige her, for she was a Londoner Born and Bred and had known every building since her childhood. The girls made good use of the shopping facilities, and Gil joked that they would soon have to return home before Fern had spent all the money needed for their fare back to Canada.

Gil's finished manuscript had been delivered to his Publisher, and they returned to the cottage once more to prepare for the return to Canada.

Shall we take Bitza for a last walk before we go? Fern suggested to Gil, the evening before their journey. As they set out, Fern said, Could we go to East Leigh House? Perhaps it might jog my memory. Are you sue you want to go there? It might bring back bad memories that you would rather forget. Gil replied looking doubtful. I'll just look from a distance that will be enough. Fern assured him. And so they set out with Bitza on a lead, and walked across the fields to Eastleigh.

Fern's attention was distracted by answering a question from Marcia, and she must not have been holding the lead tightly enough, for one moment she was holding the bouncing little dog and the next instance he was off and away across the field, his lead trailing behind him. Oh no! Fern gasped, we must catch him, he will be after Chloe, and who knows what Bennett will do if he catches him.

When they arrived in the Stable Yard at Eastleigh, they found Bitza capering about the yard, with Chloe who was gambolling around him excitedly. Bitza, come here, Bad Dog! Come here at once! Fern ordered him. But Bitza was far too excited to heed any orders. Gil was making as effort to capture Chloe, and all was pandemonium, until above the muddled sounds of barking and shouting came the loud clear crack of a gunshot. Fern collapse with Bitza in her arms. There seemed to be blood everywhere. For a frozen second nobody moved, and then all was action. . Marcia dived to catch Chloe and hold her by the collar. Gil rushed to catch Fern as she crumpled to the ground, still clasping Bitza in her arms. Bennett stood with the rifle still in his hands, he appeared to be transfixed, as if he had no idea what he had done. And it was clear that he had been drinking heavily. Fern still clasping Bitza to her chest struggled to her feet and began to scream at Bennett. You wicked evil man, to shoot a defenceless little dog just because he was playing with your stupid pet. I hate you, and I've always hated you, you were beastly to me when I was a child.

You threw me in the feed bin, because I wanted to sit in the quiet table and read. You pulled my plaits until I cried and then you were satisfied. You took my pocket money, and deliberately broke my toys, and threatened me that if I told anyone you would lock me in the cellar and not tell anyone I was there, because you knew that I was frightened of the dark. And even when I was grown up and came home to look after Father, you still bullied me. You hit me if the meals were even a little late, and even accused me of having an affair with Gil, and you pushed me so hard that I smashed my face against the wooden bed. If it hadn't been for Gil taking me to College in London, you would have ended up killing me I'm, sure. And even when I lived in London you tried to poison my friends so that I would be blamed for murder. And now you have killed Bitza You wicked Evil Brute. I wish you were dead! Instead of Bitza. A storm of weeping followed this diatribe. But Gil was too busy trying to stem the flow of blood from Fern's head and the wound on Bitza's side. Between the dog and Fern he couldn't make out which one was wounded the most.

Marcia had removed the gun from Bennett's hands, and disarmed it. She had rung 999 and an ambulance was at that moment entering the yard, followed by a police car, and thankfully order was soon restored. The Ambulance drove away with Fern and her two attendants. She wouldn't be parted from Bitza, and so he was patched up and taken with them. Bennett was taken off to the Police Station, to be charged, and put in a cell to sober up. Both

Fern and Bitza, thankfully, had only sustained flesh wounds, and although at first with their combined blood it had looked frightening, after cleansing and a dressing they found that the wounds were not so serious

Marcia was puzzled, and asked Gil. What did Fern mean when she was screaming all those accusations at Bennett? I didn't hear what she was saying; Gil replied I was too concerned that her wound might be fatal.

I didn't understand most of it, Marcia said. But it was something about a 'Child'.

Presently a nurse brought Fern in a wheel chair, her head was bandaged and she was pale and tearful. Is Bitza dead? She asked anxiously.

No, he's perfectly OK. Gil reassured her, and the vet said he'd keep him overnight just to be on the safe side. What about you? What a fright you gave me I thought that idiot had killed you or injured you badly; there was so much blood that I wasn't sure who was injured the most you or Bitza. Fern was able to leave the hospital, with instructions that if she had any problems she must be taken to A and E.immediately.

Back at the cottage, Fern was settled into an armchair. What were you shouting at Bennett when he shot at Bitza? Gil asked. I was telling him how much I had always hated him when I was a child; because of all the horrible bullying way he had repeatedly treated me.

You remember all that? Gil asked in amazement. Yes I remember everything, I don't know how it happened, but it just all came to me when I thought that he had killed Bitza. I felt the hate well up and it all came pouring out. Gil caught her up in his arms. Darling do you realise that you've recovered your memory at last. It's a miracle cure. But not one I would advise the psychiatrists to try. Later when, Fern had been examined by the doctor. He told them. Loss of memory is a mystery, which although possible, but very rarely, has been known to be cured by a deep emotional shock. Not a cure to be recommended he added with a smile.

Gil had phoned his parents with the news of Fern's miracle recovery. There were shrieks of delight from the two girls and expressions of relief from his parents.

When Fern had phoned Tessa and Bart, Tessa had burst into tears of joy, and declared, I had a weird feeling that something 'Bad' was going to happen while you were in Eastleigh.. And although something 'Bad' did happen, in a strange way it turned out to be 'Good.'

When are you coming back? Tessa asked. We'll be back tomorrow. Fern replied. I can't wait to see you all and tell you about our holiday. The weather was lovely and we're bringing Marcia with us if that's OK. She'll be travelling back to Canada with us, because she lives in Vancouver too. There's so much to tell you I can't wait to see you all, especially the babies.

The journey to Hampstead was uneventful, and their arrival was greeted with great pleasure. Especially by Marina, for although she had missed them all, she had missed Biza the most, for she didn't know that he was actually Fern's dog, and she looked upon him as her own. She was very concerned about his 'Sore Place' and insisted that her Daddy must go and see the bad man who had hurt Bitza and 'Tell him off'. When she was allowed to 'Help' Gil and Fern take Bitza to the Vet. She was delighted, and after the visit she announced that when she was a 'Lady' she too would be a 'Dog Doctor' and make all the sick animals better again.

Their journey to Canada was delayed for a couple of weeks, Because the Doctor wanted Fern to wait for a little while until the headaches she sometimes suffered had been tested.

The police had contacted Gil and Fern, asking if they wished to make an official complaint against Bennett. But Fern declined, she had seen enough of Bennett and Eastleigh, and she just wanted to be free of it all. He had spoiled her childhood; and she didn't want him to spoil anything more in her life. Bitza was safe and that was the end of it. When Fern told Tessa of the police offer. She said wisely,

You were right to refuse, revenge isn't always sweet. Bennett is his own worst enemy, and he will have to suffer the consequences of it in the end.

After a month, Fern was pronounced well enough to travel, and preparations began for their return to Canada. It was a sad parting for Fern had to leave her darling Bitza behind. He had been her only companion and comfort for a long time, when she'd had nobody to comfort her, and he was very special. But as much as she would have liked to, she knew that she couldn't take him back to Canada with her. He was better off here living here so close to the Heath, with a big closed in garden to play in, and with Marina, who would have been inconsolable if Fern had taken him away. At the airport there were many tears, hugs, kisses; and invitations to, 'Come again soon'. And then they were gone.

CHAPTER FORTEEN

Dora, Phil, Molly and Pippa all greeted them at the airport, with many hugs and kisses. You'd think we'd been away for five years, Gil joked. It seemed like it, Pippa said, especially now that Fern has regained her memory, we were longing to see her and tell her how sorry we were, and how pleased we are that she's better. Phil had borrowed a huge station wagon to transport them and the luggage, and after introducing Marcia, they all piled into the vehicle and set off home.

By coincidence, Marcia didn't live far from the Manning's and they were able to take her home. There were more introduction and 'Thankyou's and Goodbyes', they exchanged telephone numbers and at last were truly on their way home.

Later that evening as she climbed into bed, Fern said, I think I'd like to go back to our apartment tomorrow. Do you feel up to it? Gil asked in concern. I've had three months holiday and I feel fine, and now that I have my memory I feel even better. Fern replied. That's settled then. Gil said, as he switched off the light.

It seemed strange to Fern to be in her own kitchen once more. The last time she had been there she hadn't been able to remember where any thing was stored. She had been trying to bake a cake as a surprise for Gil, and became frustrated, raging at herself, thinking, I can't even remember where anything is in my own kitchen. Now she felt as if a burden had been lifted from her shoulders and she began to prepare a meal. Dora had thoughtfully stocked the fridge and freezer for them. I must remember to thank her, Fern said to herself, and began to write it down on the pad beside the phone. She hesitated for a moment; this was the pad she had used to remember things when she had amnesia. Did she need it now? And she decided that perhaps she did need it, for the time being any way.

Molly had gone to University as planned and Pippa was now in her last year at High School. In spite of their busy lives, they still found time to daydream of Ed and Nate, and wonder what they were doing and if they ever thought about them. If they had known how often both of the men had almost telephoned and declared their true feelings to the girls, they would have been amazed and delighted. Both men knew that waiting until the girls were older was the right thing to do, no matter how hard. But the path of true love was never easy. And with that they both heartily agreed.

Ed felt as if he was suffocating, he moved restlessly unable to move his arms. The whine of shells, and the crack of guns. Then, the extra boom of the exploding bombs, the painful thud as he was thrown from his vehicle by the blast of a mine. He scratched at his face trying to clear the earth from his mouth and eyes. Then he groaned and fought against restraining arms that were holding him tight. His mind cleared a little and he heard his father's voice. It's OK Son, I've got you you're safe now. Don't struggle anymore. There's help here now. Come on lad open your eyes and wake up. He felt a hand gently smoothing his brow and brushing back his hair. The arms were not restraining now, but gentle and comforting, and the loving voice kept repeating. You're safe now Son let me help you. Gradually Ed calmed down and slept. Abe seeing his son now sleeping naturally, gently released him, and lay down beside him on the bed. Hoping, that would be the last bad dream for tonight.

Abe sighed, the nightmares were getting less frequent just as the doctor had said they would, but it sure is tiring he thought, as bad as having a teething Baby.

Nate was not having nightmares, but he was counting the months until Pippa was old enough for him to ask her for a date. He had tried going out with one or two other girls but he never repeated the invitations.

Eventually he gave up and concentrated on his studies. He sent Pippa a card and some perfume for her seventeenth birthday, Pippa was delighted and treasured the gift, using the perfume sparingly to make it last as long as possible. She thought long and hard over the thank you letter. She wanted to thank Nate, but also to show him that she still thought of him. The letter he wrote to her in answer, was read and re-read, then kept in her diary, to be read again. Pippa was working hard at her studies, for she was determined to be a nurse. She knew that she wasn't clever enough to be a doctor as Nate would be, but she felt that nursing would be close.

Much to Molly's disappointment she didn't hear from Ed. She often wondered about him. Perhaps she had been mistaken when she thought that he had been as attracted to her as she was to him. She waited in vain for a letter or card when it was her eighteenth Birthday, but none came. She made plenty of friends at UNI, and plenty of dates were offered, but the boys all seemed so immature when she compared them with Ed Grant.

Ed meanwhile was struggling with his nightmares, and although he longed to call Molly and to see her again, he felt that he couldn't burden an attractive young girl with an older man, especially not a damaged veteran like him. After much thought, he decided not to do anything, and buried himself in his writing.

Fern was missing Bitza, and although she knew that she couldn't have brought him to Canada she still missed him. She happened to see a picture of a little dog exactly like him in a magazine, and mentioned it to Gil. Some weeks later on her birthday, Gil suggested that as it was a sunny day, they should go out of town for lunch. Fern happily agreed and they set out after breakfast. Where exactly are we going? Fern asked, after they had been travelling for an hour. Not far now, Gil replied. Turning down a narrow lane and then into the driveway of a large house. Here we are, he said cheerfully drawing up in front of the house. What are we doing here? Fern asked. You'll see soon enough. Have patience my love. Gil told her.

Gil knocked on the door, which was opened by a cheerful lady, who smiled at them saying. Ah! There you are. My Husband said that you had phoned to say you were on your way. And opening the door wider she welcomed then inside. I gather you've come to see our little family, they're in here, she said leading the way. Puzzled, Fern followed her into a small room leading off the kitchen, and there in the corner was a large basket containing six puppies. Their mother looked exactly like Bitza. The six little pups were a mixture.

But there was one who looked like his mother and he too was the image of Bitza. Fern fell on her knees beside the basket. Oh what a darling! She exclaimed picking up the fat little pup and hugging him, while he licked her chin. I thought you might like to choose one of the pups, but I see you've already decided which one you'd like. Gil said. Oh, he's adorable, Fern said, can I really keep him? Yes. He's yours if you want him. Fern jumped up with the puppy still in her arms and hugged Gil. Careful, don't suffocate the little chap, Gil cautioned. Can we take him home now? Fern asked excitedly. I'm, sure that Mrs Roberts would be quite happy to let you take all of them, Gil laughed, but we only have room for one. Does the puppy have a name? He asked. Mrs Roberts shook her head. I decided to let the new owners choose the names.

Then I shall call him Gem, short for Gemini, because he looks just like a twin to Bitza. Fern declared.

Mrs Roberts was very helpful and gave them a starter pack of the food that the puppy had been eating, and on the way home, they called in to a pet store to buy the necessary equipment for the puppy. Where shall we put his basket? Fern said. I suppose in the kitchen would be the best place; I can hear him from there if he cries in the night. Yes, and if he does cry in the night, he is definitely not coming into our bed. It's a bad habit and it's not hygienic. Gil replied. Bitza always slept in the stable, because Bennett wouldn't even let him into the house. Fern said sadly. We won't go that far, Gil laughed. But when he goes to bed we'll put some warm water in a bottle and put it into an old woolly sock. If we put that into his basket it will be a comfort to him and he won't feel so lonely. Let's go and show him to the family. Fern said eagerly.

As expected, Gem was petted and fussed over by Dora and the girls. Oh No! Phil gave a mock groan. You've started something, now. The girls will be pestering me for a 'cute' little puppy. Don't tell them there are five more like him, or I shall never hear the last of it.

The puppy soon settled down, and learned the simple 'rules' of living in a house, he also learned that Fern was a 'push over' and that Gil was not.

Fern's happiness was complete now, except for one thing that worried her, they had been married for several years, and there was still no sign of a baby. She had once mentioned this to Gil, and they had both gone for a test, which had proved normal. Don't worry about it, there's plenty of time yet. Gil had comforted her. And she had not mentioned it again. She didn't want to become one of those women who continually moan about their problems. But she did worry about it and constantly watched for signs, but they never happened. She had begun to call the puppy her 'baby'. I must get out of that habit she told herself, or I'll become one of those sad women who carry their little dog about in a handbag that matches their outfit.

Fern was visiting Dora one afternoon.. The girls were not there and they were able to talk freely. Suddenly, after a long pause, Dora caught Fern looking at a picture of a baby in a magazine. She had been looking at it for several minutes and her wistful expression touched Dora's sympathy. For she knew that feeling, she had experienced it herself. Having been a nurse she knew many of the pitfalls for young women who couldn't or didn't conceive and she decided that she would try her best to help Fern. But Fern hadn't confided in her and so she would have to tread carefully for no doubt it was a sore subject.

Dora decided to get as much information as possible about Fern's problem. She was surprised to find a great deal of information on the Internet. One method, which Dora liked, and which seemed to fit into Ferns situation, was Therapy. There were many to choose from, but the method that Dora liked the most, was the one with meditation and soothing Homeopathic oils. She sent off for a pamphlet and received a detailed explanation of this method. There was a number for contact and Dora used it. She found that the practitioner training took five years, and all their practitioners were fully trained. The training not only consisted of meditation and massage with the Oils, but also some psychiatry. The results given were high. The method had been invented in England, but had now spread to Italy and Germany and best of all there was a newly opened Clinic in Vancouver. Dora was pleased with the result of her research, and soon presented the facts to Fern. At first Fern had been doubtful. How could meditation or massage cure a fault in her productive system? Well it can't do any harm, Dora pointed out, and it's worth a try. I'll come with you if you like.

CHAPTER FIFTEEN

The Clinic was situated in a large office block in the centre of Vancouver. They parked underneath the building and took the lift to the appropriate floor. Fern had butterflies in her stomach and her hands were cold as ice. This is worse than going to the dentist she thought. Please come in with me, she begged Dora.

I will if they allow me. Dora assured her. Inside the Therapist room was peaceful, gentle soothing music was playing quietly in the background and Fern began to feel a little less nervous.

Juliet Hart watched the two ladies as they came in. The young one looking terrified, and the older lady looked confident. A Mother and daughter perhaps? She guessed, as she rose and held out her hand in welcome. Do sit down she said, to Fern, and then, turning to Dora she said. I shall be asking your daughter some personal questions, so perhaps you would be more comfortable in the lounge Mrs Manning. But I would like to speak to you later if I may.

When Juliet discovered that Dora was Fern's Mother-in-law, she apologised, and then moved smoothly on to begin her councelling. At the end of an hour, Fern had begun to understand the causes of her problem. She would still have to make more visits, but she was feeling more hopeful, and looked forward to her next session. Over a period of time, she learned that her childhood had caused much of her tension and fears, but now that she was in a stable marriage and was having help with her anxieties, there was the chance of a successful outcome.

After her initial nervousness, Fern enjoyed her sessions, and began to look forward to them each week. She had now reached the stage when Massage with Homeopathic oil was used. One afternoon as she lay on the Pink Massage Table, Fern thought. I'm not sure this will work as I had hoped it would. But I'm glad that I tried, I do feel less wound up and worried.

Fern had not told Gil of her Therapy sessions, for many people thought that if anything wasn't 'Medical' it must be 'Mumbo Jumbo', and not to be trusted. The fault of this thinking was sadly caused by the many who claimed to be genuine Herbalist or Homeopaths, when they were really just dabblers, without the correct knowledge. Fern especially found the relaxing techniques helpful, and practised them regularly.

After three months of weekly visits, Juliet felt that Fern was now practised enough to continue with her relaxation at home.

Fern had taken up her painting again, and was now giving classes once a week to the children in the First Grade at the local School. She enjoyed being with the children, and they became very attached to her. She now began to feel as if she were no longer a stranger in another country not her own.

Gem, was growing into a bright intelligent little dog, and as he grew, the more resemblance he had to Biza. Sometimes Fern had to check herself from calling him by that name. Each day Fern took him to a nearby Park where she met other dog owners. Some of them were the mothers of the children at school. This was a mixed blessing, for sometimes a particularly fond mother would want to tell Fern how artistic her child was, and why hadn't their painting ever been displayed on the classroom wall.

The summer had been particularly hot, and after school had closed for the three month Vacation, Gil had decided to take Fern and Gem up into the mountains where it was cooler. He hired a comfortable Camper Van. Then packing up their clothes, food and Gem's basket, they set off for a welcome rest. Gil planned to try and finish his latest book, and Fern just wanted to have a 'Holiday'.

In the mountains they found a perfect spot. With a good view, and settle down to make their camp. Gil worked at his typewriter, it wasn't as efficient as his computer, but they had no electricity for that. Fern sunbathed and read.

And in the evenings, they walked in the cool air with Gem busily looking for something to chase.

Gem had been running ahead of them, but as they turned to go back the way that they had come, there was no sign of him. Now where has that little Imp gone, Gil said calling and whistling once more, but there was still no barked reply. Something terrible has happened to him I'm sure it has, Fern said, he always barks when I call him. Calm down, he's probably too far away to hear us. Gil said. They walked on, still calling and whistling, but there was still no sign of Gem. Perhaps we're walking in the wrong direction, Fern suggested, we should have come across him by now. They tried several directions, without any success, and were about to give up in despair, when Fern suddenly halted saying. Shush! I thought I heard something. They both listened intently. Over there! Fern pointed, I'm sure it's coming from over there. Both of them ran in the direction of the barking and arrived at a large pile of rocks. Gem was barking excitedly.. He had been trying to get into a hole between the rocks; He had managed to wriggle in half way, but now couldn't get out. Naughty Gem, Fern scolded him, between tears and laughter, for Gem looked so comical with his behind sticking out from between the rocks, and his tail wagging furiously.

With some difficulty they extricated the little dog, and Fern began to brush him down with her hands, all the while scolding him for his prank. But however, when they turned to leave, Gem would not go with them, and still stood before the hole barking. What is it boy? Have you found a rabbit down there, Gil asked, Move over and let me have a look. He knelt before the hole and taking a torch from his pocket he shone it into the space. He peered into the semi darkness, but could still see nothing. Let me have a look, Fern said, I'm smaller. I might be able to lean in further. Higher up the crack widened and so far did she lean inside, that Gil was afraid she would get trapped, and he had visions of having to get the Mountain Rescue to dig her out.

Gil was just about to insist or even pull her out forcibly; when Fern said 'Wait' I can see something down there. Whatever it is, it's not worth getting trapped in the rocks to find it, come out now. He insisted. But Fern was too inquisitive to let it go, and she squeezed in a little more. For God's Fern, come out before you get stuck. Gil exclaimed.

The darkness was so black that it seemed almost solid and Fern felt that if she reached out her hand she could touch it, and she switched on the little torch. I can see something she called back. For although it was still dark a little glimmer of light showed from the torch. As her eyes became used to the darkness she could see that the tunnel had opened out into a cave. Wow, wait until I tell Pippa of this, she'll be so envious Fern said. But why had Gem been barking so madly, what was in here to disturb him? The space was small and Fern began to run her hands around the wall, then she caught her foot against something soft, she shone her torch down to the ground, and had the shock of her life. For the something soft had been a body. For a moment she froze, and then kneeling down she felt for a pulse. Dreading that there wouldn't be one. But it was there, a feint thread of a quiver, She gave a sigh of relief and squeezed her way out of the cave entrance, but she was shaking so much with cold and shock that when Gil finally pulled her out, she could hardly speak. A man in there! She gasped. What are you talking about? Gil said, come on lets get you back to the Van, your frozen. No, No, Fern protested desperately. There's a man in there and he's barely alive. What! Gil gasped, are you sure? Of course I'm sure, and if we don't act now he'll soon be dead. I'll call Mountain Rescue, Gil replied. Lets hope I can get a signal up here; otherwise he's got no chance.

Luckily Gil did get a signal and very soon the rescue team arrived. That was he easy part. The hardest was to get the man out of the hidden cave. Fern looked around her at all the men, None of you will be able to get in there, and he needs a harness, so it looks as if I shall have to go in again. Although Gil protested, Fern shook her head. What else can we do? None of you could get in there, and I'm guessing that the crooks thought that they had finished him. Lets go and prove them wrong. Give me the harness and I'll do my best. Then taking the leather straps, she once more slid into the hole between the rocks. At least it's on the level and I don't have to climb or be lowered into it. She thought. Now that she had a brighter torch she was able to work faster, she struggled but at last had the harness on the man's body. She gave the signal to haul and helped to guide him over any lumps. By the time he had been heaved and pulled out into the sunshine, Fern wondered if the poor man was still alive. He must have been made of stern stuff, for his pulse was still beating weakly, in spite of the rough treatment. After exchanging names and addresses, The Helicopter rose into the air and disappeared over the brow of the hills

Well! Fern exclaimed, who would have thought a simple camping holiday could have been so exciting. It might have been exciting for you, Gil said. But I was terrified that there might be a rock fall and you could have been crushed or trapped and I would have lost you. He hugged her tightly; please don't give me a shock like that again. He begged.

Gem, having been the initial cause of the affair, had now curled up into a ball and gone to sleep. Ah, Bless him! Fern said looking at him fondly. He's worn out after so much excitement. Not half as worn out as I am with the fright you gave me Gil replied, and scooping the puppy up under his arm, then putting his other arm around Fern's shoulder he guided them back to their Camp.

For the rest of the time they had a lazy holiday, Gil re-typing his book and checking to see if any corrections were needed. While Fern put up her easel and painted scenery, She did a painting of Gem, while he was sleeping, there was no chance when he was awake, he would never stay still long enough. But at last it was time to go home.

I'm sad to be going home, Fern said, but glad too, Holidays are lovely, but there's no place like home is there?

CHAPTER SIXTEEN

Greg Foster, had lain unconscious for some hours, and the nurses had been checking him regularly. He groaned, thinking why can't I move? I feel as if a herd of buffalo have tramped over me. He groaned once more and opened his eyes. Above him he saw a pair of bright blue eyes, a halo of golden curls and a sweet face, which was looking at him anxiously. Are you an Angel? He asked. The sweet anxious look turned into a grin. I can see your feeling better already Mr Foster. The nurse replied. Beginning to take his pulse. It s no good doing that Greg protested, it's gone up several degrees since I saw you.

The nurse smiled, she was used to cheeky remarks from the men on the wards no matter what their age. But this one she didn't mind, for some reason she felt akin to him for she had once been 'beaten up' herself and she knew how traumatic it felt both physically and mentally. She took his temperature, gave him a drink of water and left him alone once more.

Greg looked around the room; there were no flowers or cards to be seen. Well I hardly expected them, he thought, for who knows or cares that I'm here? In that he was mistaken, for his superior officer was very interested, and had been impatiently waiting for him to regain consciousness so that he could be questioned, because he knew the information that Greg had gathered was important to the case on which they had been working. Greg frowned trying to gather his thoughts together. He had not made notes, fearing that the crooks would guess who he was. They had still suspected him, and decided to get rid of him, but by some miracle he had survived, he didn't know how, but he intended to find out if he could.

When his Superior came to visit him. The Nursing Sister refused him admittance, saying that an official document must be shown, for Mr Foster was officially under police protection. Eventually the correct document was produce and the now 'Irate' visitor was admitted.

Greg was dozing when D.I Gould stomped crossly into his room, for he was not used to young women challenging his official authority. Greg grinned. What's the matter, Guv? Have you met your match? That Sister is a real Tarter; you don't want to get on the wrong side of her. Greg advised. Gould grunted, Never mind her, what information did you manage to get?

When Greg had recounted his findings, Gould whistled, no wonder they wanted to get rid of you, this Intelligence could get them a long stretch.. When will you be back? I need you on this case. Better ask the Sister that question. Greg replied with a grin, but I don't rate your chances. You seem to have upset her; I wonder how you did that? He said wryly. Gould snorted, B***** bossy woman thinks she's in charge of everything. That's because she is. Greg grinned. At least she is in here anyway.

The injuries that Greg had sustained proved to be more serious than at first supposed and his stay in hospital was longer than expected. Another undercover agent was assigned to Gould, who continually complained that he was not as good as Greg. Lying in hospital gave Greg time to think about his future and he began to feel that the undercover work was no longer for him.

The pretty little nurse, who had been there when he had first woken up, had at first been assigned to him. But now that he was no longer on the danger list, she had been moved on to another 'at risk' patient. Greg missed her pretty face and sweet smile, and although the older nurse who now tended him was kind and caring, she was still not his' Angel'. She brightened my day, but now I never see her, he thought sadly.

Greg's 'Angel' had been on nights for several days. But now, much to her relief, she was to be put back onto the daytime Roster. Consequently, when Greg was least expecting her she came in to change his dressings. Oh Boy! Am I glad to see you he exclaimed? You've no idea how much I've missed your smiling face. I'm sure Nurse Grey has been looking after you just as well as I would. She replied. Yes she was a great nurse, but she wasn't 'You'. He declared.

As the days went by Greg realised that he was falling in love with his 'Angel', Am I even allowed by hospital ethics to fall in love with my nurse, he thought. And I'm sure she's not allowed to fall in love with a patient. But since she shows no interest in me. I guess it doesn't matter. Greg was wrong in thinking the

Pretty nurse had not noticed the handsome patient in room seven. In spite of his injuries, which must have been unbearably painful, he was always cheerful and never complained, and something that she really appreciated, was the fact that although she could tell that he was attracted to her, he never made suggestive innuendos or jokes, as many male patients were prone to do.

Greg's 'Angel'. Was beginning to feel anything but angelic towards her patient, infact she was falling in love with him, and she knew that it was foolish to do so, for presently he would be going back to his own world, with friends and colleagues, and he would soon forget her in his busy exciting life. She was wrong in thinking that would be the case. For Greg had been lying for long hours alone in hospital he'd had few visitors, His work colleagues were busier than ever, especially now that he was gone, and although the case he had worked on had now been completed and the crooks jailed, there were many more cases waiting to be dealt with.

He had no close relatives for he had been an only child of parents who were themselves only children. And so there were no siblings or aunts and uncles to comfort him. It had never bothered him before, but now he felt the loss. It would have been nice to have someone, apart from the Hospital Staff to care if he lived or died.

Now that the girls were more settled at college and University. Dora felt that she would like to do something for herself, something outside the home where she would meet people and be helpful. She had always been good at socialising, and had regularly helped at the School Jumble Sales, Bazaars and any other socialising. One of her friends had joined the hospital League of Friends, and Dora felt that would be just the job for her, especially as it was only part time.

On her first morning in the Hospital Shop, a young nurse came in and asked for a book for a young male patient. What kind of book does he like Dora asked? I don't know the girl replied, but I know that he lead a dangerous life, he was badly injured when he was admitted. Dora offered her a paperback, it was one of Gil's stories and she guessed that it would appeal to a young man. The young nurse thanked her, saying that she would let her know if the patient liked the book, Dora smiled to herself, little did the girl know that in Hard Back it had been a best seller, and it was written by Dora's son.

Greg was grateful for the book, although he had never had much spare time to read, he had read some of the other books by this author and had enjoyed them, and he settled down to read this one. The nurse, satisfied that he was comfortable, left him to read in peace He must have been a speedy reader for the nurse came back several times for more books by the same author, until Dora said regretfully that those were all the books they had by him, and would the patient like to try another Author.

During his long hours alone Greg practiced his Physio movements, and had begun to get on to his feet, but this was only allowed when he was accompanied by one of he staff. He also daydreamed about what he would do when he finally came out of hospital. Many of the Daydreams included the young nurse, although he felt he had little hope of them ever coming true. One thing he had definitely decided was that he was not going back to the undercover intelligence work. This was his third spell in hospital, and it had been the longest. He felt that he'd had enough and was ready for a change. I'm not getting any younger, and I can't go on being 'Action Man' forever he told himself. For sometime he had been thinking over plans for his future and had made a decision. He would hand in his notice right away. And when he was discharged from hospital he would go back to the profession that he had been trained for.

When he was eighteen he had gone to University and trained as a Lawyer. When he had qualified he'd worked in a practice that dealt mostly with domestic run- of- the mill work, such as Wills, Conveyance and petty squabbles between neighbours. Now he decided he would do Criminal Law, even if it meant going back to College for a while, he could afford it for he had been paid an excellent salary, and he had spent little of it, because he was always chasing off after criminals. Now the Criminals would come to him for help. He felt well pleased with his decision, and picking up his phone, he began to make arrangement for the start of his new life.

The young nurse who had been caring for Greg, had been away on a weeks leave, When she returned she went to room seven, expecting to see her usual patient, but to her consternation there was an elderly lady in room seven. When she hurried to the nursing station to enquire where Mr.Foster had been taken. She was told that he had discharged himself, and would be an outpatient in future. At first she couldn't believe that he would leave without saying goodbye, for she felt that there had been something special between them, but perhaps she had been wrong. She tried to forget about it, and went on with her duties.

Greg had hoped that 'His nurse' as he called her would have been back on duty before he left, he was disappointed when she didn't return in time, but he couldn't delay his departure, for he had an important interview at the College, which he couldn't miss. Each time he attended the outpatients for his check up, he hoped to see her, he even went up to room seven, but she was off duty that day. It seemed as if fate didn't want them to meet again.

When he had been given his discharge papers at the hospital, he asked the sister if she had any record of the person who had found him in the cave. There was no record in his file, but the Sister said that she knew the people who had found him. Their mother works in the 'Friends' shop downstairs. She told him.

Greg went to the shop immediately, but it was not Dora's day to be there. Greg was disappointed, but he refused to give up and wrote a note to her with his phone number, explaining his reason for contacting her.

He waited anxiously, and a few days later Dora phoned him and they made arrangements to meet.

Greg couldn't wait; at last he would be able to thank the people who had helped to save him.

CHAPTER SEVENTEEN

Dora had been pleased to get the note from Greg, and was keen to meet him. Fern was excited too; she had hoped to eventually meet the man she had rescued, and was curious to see what he was like and to find out how he had come to be there in the cave. She waited eagerly for Greg to arrive, and when she saw him, she was amazed, for he was tall and very good-looking. His dark hair curled attractively round his collar and a curl fell forward on is forehead. His dark eyes surveyed her seriously but his smile and handshake were both warm as he said in a pleasantly soft Scottish brogue, I've been wanting to meet you and thank you for your brave rescue. Oh, you're Scottish! Fern exclaimed. And you're English, Greg replied as he released her hand to shake Gil's. I came here to get married, Fern explained. And I came to find a more exciting job. Greg replied. Well, you certainly found one that turned out to be more exciting than you expected, Gil said. Dora came bustling in with tea and home made cake. It's a long time since I had home made cake, Greg remarked. I'll give you some to take home, Dora replied. You boys all like cake, I know.

Fern and Gil were both keen to hear how Greg had come to be attacked. It was because of my job, Greg explained.

I was an under cover agent with the police. We had tracked a gang of thieves and we needed more information, and evidence, and so I posed as one of them. I had done it quite a few times, but that time was one time too many and I was discovered. They beat me up and one of them wanted to kill me, but the others refused, They didn't want to go as far as murder, incase they did get caught, which of course is what happened. If you hadn't found me, they would definitely have been charged with murder.

Will you change your job now? Fern asked him. I'm going back to College. I was a qualified Lawyer before I went into the police, thinking, as young men do, that it would be more interesting. It was certainly that, but as you can see it was dangerous too. Greg replied. As he was talking, Fern thought, with those eyes of his, he could glare at a criminal and they would feel as if he could see right into their mind. They chatted for a while, and eventually Greg said that he must go for he had an appointment.

I'm so happy that it all turned out well, and you are really on the mend. I hope you don't get any long term effects, Dora said solicitously, and you must come and see us again, you know, they say if you save someone's life you will be friends forever. That would be nice wouldn't it? Yes it would Greg replied, I'll look forward to seeing you all again. I expect your mother is pleased that you have changed your job, Dora said. She must have been so concerned about you, and then that terrible attack too, poor woman, she must have been so worried.

I'm afraid I don't have a mother Mrs Manning. My parents are both dead, I don't have any siblings, or grandparents, and not even aunts and uncles. So you see I shall be glad of new friends. Oh you poor boy! Dora exclaimed. Well, you're always welcome to visit us, she said, giving him a hug, before he left.

The telephone rang shrill and loud, Gil who was in the middle of trying to finish his latest book,, swore under his breath, and called to Fern, Could you answer that please Honey. If it's for me, tell them I'll ring back later. The ringing ceased and Gil heard Fern say, Hi! I was going to ring you and you've beaten me to it. Her voice faded as she closed the door and settled down to chat with her friend.

Presently she brought Gil a cup of coffee. That was Marcia on the phone; she's coming round this afternoon.

That's nice, Gil replied absently, and Fern decided to leave him to his work.

Have you been busy at the hospital, Fern asked Marcia as she handed her a cup of tea and set a plate of cakes near her. It hasn't been too bad, Marcia replied. But it will be, come the winter, it's always worse then. With illness and falls on the icy sidewalks. How is your 'Special' patient getting on? Fern asked, She was interested, for Marcia had told her of him when he had first been brought into the Hospital. He was next-door to dead, Marcia had said, and they thought that they had lost him a couple of times. The doctors were amazed and said that he must have a very strong constitution, or else a Lucky Star, for against all odds he has survived. Is he up and about now? Fern asked. He's more than that, Marcia replied. When I came back on duty after a three-day break, I found that he had discharged himself. Good heavens! Fern exclaimed, had he given you any indication that he was going to do anything so rash? As far as I can make out it was a spur of the moment decision on his part, and he couldn't be swayed. Apparently he said that he was about to start a new way of life. Well, Fern said, I suppose if his old life lead to him being practically beaten to death, then a 'New way of Life' was a good decision to make.

Marcia didn't tell Fern how hurt she had felt when she found that Greg had left the hospital without saying goodbye to her. She'd thought they had a rapport together, and had hoped that it could have developed into something more permanent. But obviously I read the signs wrongly she thought sadly, I guess when you're desperately ill, you do get somewhat attached to your carer, for you're dependent on them and grateful for any kindness. She had managed to put her disappointment to one side, but talking about him to Fern had reminded her. Marcia couldn't stay long for she was going on duty at six o'clock. They said their 'Goodbyes' but didn't disturb Gil. Give him my best. Marcia said with a smile. I don't' want to disturb him when he's working. After Marcia had gone, Fern thought. What a pity it was that such a sweet natured, pretty girl like Marcia was so alone. She has no family, and she seems to avoid men and refuses to go out on dates. After the horrible time she had with Bennett, no wonder she's wary of men. But there are lots of lovely men out there. Look at Greg; he's such a sweetie. Greg! That's the answer, why didn't I think of it before. I'll hatch a little 'Romance' plan. Those two were made for each other I know it,

When later, she told Gil of her idea., and her intention to 'Plan a Romance', he looked doubtful. Be careful what you do. Your plan could turn into a disaster, and then what will you do to put it right.

Fern thought for some time before she could think of a way to get Marcia and Greg together, or even for them to meet. She had to be careful not to make it look too obvious. She discarded one plan after another and she was at a loss to think of something. Then one afternoon when Marcia had visited her, they had talked about a Musical Show that Fern and Gil wanted to see at the Local Theatre. Marcia had said that she would have liked to go and see it but didn't want to go alone. Fern asked when Marcia's next off duty times were. Now all she had to do was discover when Greg was free. She rang Greg and asked him if he would like to go and see the Musical, He agreed, and Fern said. You can come with us. It's nicer than going on your own. The date was agreed and Fern booked four tickets. She hadn't told Gil, she knew that he would be full of warnings. I know I'm taking a risk, Fern thought. And I'm not 'tricking' them. She told herself. Just 'guiding' them in the right direction. As the date drew near, she became nervous and a little worried too that her' Romantic Plan' wouldn't work, Supposing Gil was right and her actions might be construed as 'Meddling'. Well it's too late now, she thought. I've burnt my boats, and there's no way out.

On the night of the Theatre outing, Fern had continual butterflies in her stomach, and could hardly stop thinking of all the things that could go wrong. At last they were on their way. They had arranged to meet Greg and, unknown to the men, Marcia too, inside the Theatre, Fern had sent tickets to Marcia and Greg, incase of hold ups. Fern trembled a little when they reached the Theatre; and looked around anxiously for either of the other two. They were actually seated in their seats when Marcia arrived, full of apologies. Fern assured her that she was in plenty of time for the Safety Curtain had not yet been raised. There was one empty seat next to Marcia, and she remarked to Fern. It's a good thing that seat is on the end of the row, and not in the middle, or the person who is going to be late, wouldn't be very popular with the other people in the row. Fern laughed nervously, and said jokingly, but it's a good seat for going to get the ice cream before the queue gets too long. Several times Fern looked behind her up the aisle, to see if Greg had arrived. Presently the lights began to dim and the Orchestra struck up a medley of the tunes from the Show. The curtain was just going up when someone slid quietly into the seat beside Marcia. She didn't turn to see who it was, for she was concentrating on the Stage. When the lights were raised for the Interval, the man on the end stood up immediately, saying I'll get the ice creams. And he was gone before anyone could protest. Coming back shortly with four tubs of ice cream. He leaned forward and handed two to Fern then he bent to Marcia, about to say apologetically, I hope you like Vanilla it was all they had. The words were never spoken, for when he saw who had sat beside him for the last hour, he was speechless. Then he asked. Where did you spring from? I've been here all the time. Marcia replied. But the lights were going down when you arrived and it was too dark to see. Giving a sigh of relief that everything was going to plan, Fern asked innocently. Do you two know each other? This young lady was my personal nurse while I was ill. Greg explained, and an excellent job she did too. I don't know what I would have done without her. I had to leave the Hospital in a rush, while she was off duty, and when I came back she had gone and they wouldn't tell me where, They said it was against hospital policy to give out the whereabouts of Staff.

As the lights dimmed, they all settled down to enjoy the rest of the show. Later, as the audience filtered out of their seats, talking and jostling their way out of the theatre, Greg managed to keep Marcia in sight, and offered her a lift home, or to work, if that was more convenient for her. Marcia wanted to accept, but she hesitated. Fern didn't want her plan to fail and said at once. I'm sure you would be glad of a lift home wouldn't you Marcia? Especially now that it's started to rain. At that moment the rain, which had been a slight drizzle suddenly began to rain in earnest. I'll ring you tomorrow. Fern promised Marcia, as she ran for the car. That was a very unsubtle move. Gil remarked. I hope they weren't embarrassed. Well, Marcia didn't refuse to go with Greg, did she? Fern replied. You didn't give her much choice Honey, it was a case of going along with it, or refuse and cause embarrassment. Well it achieved the object of the exercise; someone had to give them some help. 'He who hesitates is lost' you know. Yes and 'Look before you leap' is another wise saying that you might consider too, Gil replied with a smile.

CHAPTER EIGHTEEN

It seemed that Fern had been correct in her feeling that Marcia and Greg only needed a little help to get them together. For after that evening they were hardly ever apart. During the drive to Marcia's flat, Greg had explained the reason for his hurried departure from the Hospital. He had been offered a position in a prestigious firm of Criminal Lawyers. Another candidate had been considered, but Greg had first place; if he could go at once. The other applicant had to serve out his notice. Greg couldn't see why he had to stay in the hospital when he could be an Out Patient, and so he had discharged himself. He still had to go to College one day a week, but because of his previous employ as an undercover agent, he was considered to be better able to deal with hardened criminals. I asked for you at the Hospital, but they wouldn't give me any help, he explained. No they wouldn't, Marcia replied, it's against Hospital policy to give details of staff, unless it is for official reasons. So they told me, Greg said. But I found it pretty frustrating, because I really wanted us to get to know each other better, or even more that better it you agreed. Oh I heartily agree, Marcia said smiling, and Greg did what he had wanted to do ever since he had first seen her. He kissed her. We'll have to get together now, Greg said. Otherwise Fern will never forgive us after all the trouble she's gone to, in trying to make us into a couple.

They spent a great deal of time together, telling each other of their past. Greg explained that when he had lived in Scotland as a boy, his father had been a Lawyer, and he had thought that was the career for him. But he found the work boring, and making Wills, and Property conveyance dry as dust. And so he had come to Canada and managed to join the police. Later, he had volunteered to be an under cover agent. It had been dangerous, but never boring. He had been in many near miss scrapes. But this one had been the last straw, and he felt that it was time to bow out and let the younger chaps have a chance.

If I hadn't gone into that line of work, we would never have met, so although it was dangerous, and as a consequence of my being beaten, I was in Hospital, We met! How's that for the mysteries of fate. I'm so glad that you've given up the under cover work, Marcia said. I would be a nervous wreck worrying about you. That's why not many of the lads are married. I'm not married yet, but hopefully I soon will be. He grinned at Marcia's surprised look. Well, you are going to marry me aren't you? Please. He said with an engaging smile. Marcia laughed. Of course I will, she said, hugging him, and when Greg kissed her she knew that she had found her true-life Partner.

Fern woke one morning and rushed to the bathroom. Oh no, it must have been that fancy foreign restaurant we tried last night. I knew it was a mistake to go there, but Marcia said they had enjoyed the meal there so much. After a while she felt a little better, and went down to the kitchen and put on the kettle. Presently Gil came into the room. Are you OK Honey? He asked. You were in a rush this morning. I'm all right now, but I think that meal last night must have upset my stomach. Yes it was pretty unusual; I guess it takes time for your stomach to get used to the exotic foods.

The next morning the same upset was repeated, and on the third morning, Gil said, 'Right' this morning you're going to see the doctor. Fern protested but Gil was adamant. The visit to the doctor was a surprise to them both. After examining her, the doctor said. You are perfectly fit Mrs Manning, You don't have a stomach bug, but you are actually pregnant. For a moment Fern couldn't believe him. But he assured her that it was definitely true. And walking on air she left the surgery to tell Gil the wonderful and exciting news.

Shall we keep it secret for a little while, just in case it's a false alarm Fern suggested. You could try, Gil said. But if I know anything about my Mom, she'll know before you have the chance to hide it. She seems to have a radar for secrets, we could never keep any when we were kids, for Mom always seemed to guess what was going on, Goodness knows how. But perhaps being a Mom gives them second sight so that they can protect their offspring. OK We'll tell your Mum, but nobody else. Gill laughed. Once you've told Mom, you won't need to tell anyone else, she'll do it for you. As Gil had predicted, when they had told Dora their good news, it wasn't long before everyone knew about it too.

The family joy knew no bounds. Even the neighbours were infected with it. For many of them had wondered if perhaps Fern could not have children, and had felt sympathy for her. Now they joined in the family's happiness.

After her initial discomfort, Fern found that she was able to carry on as usual for several months; She had her regular checks and Anti-natal Classes. This isn't as bad I thought it would be she congratulated herself. Until one night she awoke with a nagging pain in her back. She tossed about but couldn't get comfortable. And sliding out of bed intending to go to the bathroom, she felt a gush of fluid running down her nightgown. I must stay calm she scolded herself, and calmly began to get dressed. But before she could do so, another pain hit her and she doubled up with a loud groan. Gil was awake in an instant, stay where you are he said, and grabbing the phone he dialled Emergency. In the ambulance Fern felt as if the vehicle had hit every bump in the road that it was possible to find. But at last they had arrived and the nurse was wheeling her away to the maternity ward. While Gil followed carrying Fern's bag and anxiously hoping that all would be straightforward and not prolonged. Unfortunately for Fern, Gil's wish was not fulfilled. It was a long night and after a struggle, the Doctors deciding that Fern could take no more took her away for an emergency caesarean section, and delivered a beautiful baby boy, weighing eight pounds. Never had Fern and Gil been so relieved and overjoyed to hear a baby's lusty cries. It was almost as if he was indignant at being wrenched from his cosy home.

Back in her room once more, Fern held her precious baby in her arms, and Gil leaned down kissing her and then gently kissing the top of the baby's head. Thank you for our son, my brave girl. He said.

Before the baby had arrived there had been many suggestions of a name for it. But Fern and Gil had already made up their minds. And on the nametag of his hospital crib was written, Simon Gilmore Manning.

Pippa was now twenty and was in her last year of midwifery training at the hospital .She loved her job, and had been very interested and helpful to Fern when she had been pregnant. Both Pippa and Molly were to be Godmothers to the new baby. Dora couldn't wait for Fern to come home so that she could fuss over the baby. She produced photographs of Gil as a baby, to show how much the baby resembled his Daddy.

At the hospital there was to be a new Gynaecologist, and the nurses were wondering what he would be like.

Would he be young or not. They didn't even know his name.

Every birthday, Pippa had received a birthday card and short letter, from Nate Grant. They never had the chance to meet, for the Hospital and University they were each attending were at each end of the country. Pippa had never forgotten her feelings for Nate, and he remained her ideal Beau. Nobody in her eyes was good enough when compared to him. Nate too was still convinced that Pippa was his ideal and that no other girl would do.

He was looking forward to his new job, and the fact that it was in Vancouver was deliberate, for he would be able to go and visit Pippa. He knew the law about minors, and so he had kept at a distance from her, because she was a young girl if sixteen, and he was nearly twenty years old. He was at the beginning of his medical studies, and Pippa had to finish her education. Letting her go was one of the hardest things he had ever done, especially because he knew that Pippa was attracted to him in spite if her youth. His one concession to his self-imposed rule had been the yearly birthday cards with a brief greeting of good wishes. He had hoped that these would help to keep their contact open. Now that he was qualified and had a job, he was hoping that the twenty years old Pippa was still as attracted to him, as she had been when she was a child of sixteen.

Hurry up Pippa, we should be on the wards in five minutes, you know how fussy Sister Prior is if we're even a second late. You're such a 'neat nick' Mandy why is it you never have any trouble with your cap, and mine won't stay on properly. I've run out of bobby pins now, and I'm sure it will drop off and fall under sister Prior's feet. Here take a couple of mine her friend urged her; only do hurry up for goodness sake.

As they hurried along the corridor, Mandy said. That new 'Gynie' is starting this morning. I wonder what he's like. I hope he's a 'Dream Boat', but knowing our luck, he'll probably be some dry as dust old professor. They reached the ward just as Sister was arriving and hurriedly went to their allotted stations. Sister frowned at them and Pippa hoped that she wasn't frowning at her white starched cap.

The nurses waited expectantly, and when the Consultant entered followed by his train of young doctors, Pippa held her breath. But when they all halted and gathered around the first bed in the ward, Pippa had a shock. Surely that couldn't be Nate. If it wasn't, then it was someone who looked very like an older version of him. The nurses stood respectfully while the consultant spoke to Sister. The junior doctors remained silent, unless they were asked a question. Pippa's attention was on the man who looked so much like Nate. Suddenly he noticed Pippa and he did a double take, his attention had been distracted just as the Consultant asked him a question. But he must have managed to answer satisfactorily for the Consultant nodded.

Nate couldn't believe his eyes; he hadn't dreamed that he had chosen the same hospital where Pippa was training. What a bonus, he thought. But I have to be careful, a Doctor and a Student nurse could cause a scandal and Pippa would be dismissed. Pippa saw no more of Nate on the wards. But when she went home for her three-day break, there was a letter waiting for her. It was from Nate asking her to write to his lodging address, so that they could meet away from the Hospital. She wrote a reply inviting him to her home to meet her family. He already knew Molly, and she, as well as Pippa, wanted to meet and hear all his news. The meeting was a great success. Dora was at last able to thank Nate for his kindness to the girls, especially over the bullying and harassment Pippa had suffered from Lenny Small. Nate told them that Lenny had gone to a Detention Centre and then on to Rehabilitation, and was now quite a Model Citizen. He'd had a drunken father, whose bad behaviour had been copied by his son. And once removed from that situation he had learned to be more civilised.

CHAPTER NINETEEN

Nate had ventured to tell Pippa how he felt and she had returned his confidence with her own, and they were happily planning their future together.

Molly was now teaching in First Grade at the Junior School. She loved to teach the little ones, for they were still at the stage of 'My teacher says' and were eager to learn new things. As they moved further up the school grades they became more unruly and inclined to think they knew better than the teacher.

Molly was pleased for Pippa, when Nate unexpectedly re-appeared into her life. She liked him and felt that he would always be a good reliable and loving husband for Pippa, who was inclined to sometimes make impulsive decisions. She held out little hope of hearing from Ed again. For unlike Nate he hadn't sent a Birthday Card each year and not even a Christmas card. She had spoken to Abe on the phone, and knew that Ed was still at the Farm, and had not gone back to his 'War Correspondent' work. Abe, like most men was not a chatty person, and so apart from knowing that they were both well and keeping busy, she knew no more.

One of the young supply teachers at school had asked her out. She had gone out with him once, and then only because Pippa had urged her to go. You're becoming a real hermit. Pippa had chided her sister. If you don't go out you'll never meet anyone suitable. But I don't want to meet anyone, Molly insisted, I'm quite OK as I am. Molly had developed into the family beauty, not in the glamorous film star style. But she had a far more lasting attraction. Her serene classical looks often made people in the street, turn to look as she passed. But Molly had no great opinion of her looks and was completely unaware of their admiring glances.

On her twenty-first Birthday she received a parcel in the post. She didn't recognise the writing and opened it wondering curiously where it had come from. Inside the wrapping she found a hard backed book. She turned it over, and looked at the front cover and title. The printed cover had. Grey, white and red swirls like smoke and out of the centre sprang the words. 'The Hungry Machine'. Enclosed with the book was a 21st birthday card, which was signed simply. From 'Ed' Molly was puzzled, Why had Ed sent this strange apparent birthday gift and card to her? She opened the front cover and read the Flyleaf. Then all was explained. For it read. 'This book is dedicated to Molly. She was the one person that believed in me and insisted that I should write down these memories, to show how the brave men and women of our forces suffered and died to help save a helpless severely oppressed people from the 'Hungry Machine' of war and aggression. There was also a newspaper cutting, saying that the book had become a 'Best Seller' Molly couldn't help the tears forming in her eyes and spilling down her cheeks. What is it Honey Dora asked in alarm? Is it bad news, has something happened to Abe? No it's from Ed. He's written a book.

Molly said, handing her mother the book and card. Well I Never! Dora exclaimed. Whatever next?

The whole family read the book, and Molly and Dora had shed tears over its vivid descriptions of bravery and suffering. I wouldn't be surprised if that book won an award. Phillip remarked when he had read it. It's so well described that you almost feel that you are there. Molly thought for a long time if she should write to Ed, and thank him for the book and card. She didn't know what to say. She knew what she wanted to say, but did Ed want to hear it, that was the problem. Eventually she wrote a polite note, to thank him and say how much they had all liked his book. She also congratulated him on it's becoming a Best Seller. There was no reply to this missive, although Molly waited for several weeks. Molly was puzzled by the silence. Was Ed ill? Or was it because he didn't want to correspond with her. If that was so, then why had he sent her the book and card?

Eventually, she decided to write to Abe, and ask him if he and Ed were well. And was it convenient for her to visit them during the Summer Vacation from school. She received a letter from Abe, almost by return post. Saying how pleased he was that she had suggested a visit. And he would be glad of her sensible help. For what he was going to do with Ed he didn't know. He's not happy, but he say's there is nothing wrong. Abe had written. But I know he's not himself. I'll be glad of your help to sort him out. Molly phoned Abe, and they made arrangements for her to visit, as soon as the school vacation began.

Molly set off to Alberta to visit Abe. She smiled to herself remembering how she and Pippa had first gone there; they had travelled in great discomfort. But this time she went in comfort and the journey didn't seem nearly so long. Abe had arranged for Todd Ford from the garage to meet her at the station and bring her to the Farm. Todd was amazed when he saw this beautiful young woman descend from the train. Wow! He thought, what a 'looker! She had been a very pretty girl, but now she was an extremely beautiful woman.

As Todd drove her to the farm they chatted about the Little Town, and the people that Molly had known. He said that Dolly still owned the Diner, but she now had one of her nieces working there and was hoping to train her so that when Dolly retired she could leave it in her niece's capable hands. The most surprising news of all, was that Lenny Small had trained as a youth worker, and was now working with Millie Stuart the Youth Liaison Officer, he was also at college training to be a Liaison Officer himself. Molly was amazed, but also pleased to hear that at least someone had got his life sorted out, for she was not looking forward to the coming confrontation with Ed.

Abe had not told Ed of Molly's impending visit, and when he heard a car draw up in front of the house, he wondered who it could be. They seldom had a visitor, unless it was the Padre, and he rode a cycle in the summer, keeping his car only for use in the winter weather. He knew that his father had gone out with one of the 'ladies' from the church that flocked around him making sure that he was well cared for. Abe enjoyed the company, although he was perfectly capable of looking after himself. But now that Ed suffered less from his nightmares, Abe had more energy to spend time going out.

At the knock on the kitchen door, Ed sighed and switched his computer on to 'Save'. Then reluctantly went downstairs to see who was knocking. He opened the door, about to ask, Can I help you? But the words died in his throat. For there stood the mot beautiful woman he had ever seen. She remained, looking at him for a moment, and then she said nervously. 'Hullo Ed'. For a moment He stared at this vision not recognising her. When she smiled shyly at him, with the smile that had been haunting his dreams ever since the first time he had seen it. He said, Molly? The vision nodded, are you going to invite me in? She replied. Ed still in shock, said, Oh, I beg your pardon, of course. He widened the door and stood back for her to pass. As she did so he caught a drift of the soft flowery perfume he remembered she had always worn. He remembered too, that it had remained on some of the pillows for weeks after she had returned to Vancouver, and he felt his stomach tighten. Don't go there! He warned himself sternly No good will come of it. To Ed's relief, the sound of a motor vehicle drawing up outside the house, proved to be the return of Abe, and Ed asked her if she would she like to go out and meet his father who was no doubt expecting her. Molly reluctantly decided that at the moment there was going to be no explanation from Ed, but she was determined that before too long there would be plenty. Her family would have recognised the set of that firm little chin, and known that Molly was now set on the start of one of her 'Projects'. And they would have told Ed. 'Give up. 'You've got no chance Buddy'.

Abe was delighted to find that Molly had already arrived, and he hugged her saying, 'It's so great to see you Little Maid, it's been too long, and I'm not getting any younger you know? He joked. You'll never be old even when your ninety-nine, Molly said, returning his hug. Haven't you put the kettle on yet Ed? Abe chided his son. Where's your manners, the poor Maid must be gasping for a cup of tea.

The teacups were handed round, and Abe brought out the cake tin. Are you baking cakes now Abe? Molly joked. No Maid, not me, it's the Church ladies they always make sure the tin is full. Ever since you girls left.

They've done that, just because I joked one day that I missed you girls, and also the cakes that you used to bake. Ed sat silent, not joining in the banter. He was surprised; His father seemed like a different person, one that he didn't recognise. He was definitely responding towards the influence of a female in the house. Or was it only because it was Molly? Ed felt a stab of jealousy, 'Don't go there' he told himself. She owes you nothing, so don't start feeling possessive just because you—Because I what? Ed asked himself. But he wouldn't admit his feelings not even to himself.

The weather was bright and warm. We haven't had such a good summer since you and Pippa were here Abe vowed. I don't know about that Molly replied, but it's certainly lovely, after the cold winter we had.

Did you have deep snow? We did He replied. I wondered how you were getting into town for supplies. Molly said. It was no bother; Todd Ford brought me the supplies. He has a horse and sleigh. It was his fathers Sleigh.

In the old days most people round here had one. But with the modern machinery they went out of use. They chatted for a while catching up on their long absence, until suddenly Molly realised that Ed had slipped away un-noticed, as they had been talking.

She felt a twinge of annoyance. What's the matter with the man has he no manners? But then she remembered her own behaviour in the past months, How often had she slipped away to her room when the family had been talking and joking and she had felt no part of it, for she had been too deep in her own negative feelings. Well she had managed to dig herself out of her despondency, and now she was going to help Ed to come out of his, whether he wanted to not.

Molly began to gather her things together preparing to go out to the Bunk House as she had done when she was here before. But Abe checked her. No Maid, you'll be up in the back bedroom, can't have you sleeping out there alone, what if a Hobo came by in the night and decided to 'Doss' in there, there's no knowing what might happen. But I was out there before, Molly protested. Yes, but you had Pippa with you then, so it was safer with two of you. No matter how much Molly exclaimed that she had no wish to turn Ed out of his own bedroom, Abe was adamant and wouldn't be swayed. When she went upstairs to the back bedroom, she found that the bed had been changed with clean sheets, and Ed's computer and belongings had gone. Leaving a space in the wardrobe for her clothes. He must have gone up the fire escape and prepared the room while she had been downstairs talking to Abe.

CHAPTER TWENTY

In Spite of Molly's misgivings that Ed might be offended at having given up his room, Ed was infact pleased. He had a chair and a table to use while he was working, a bunk to sleep in, toilet facilities, and most important of all a place where he could shut himself away and not be bothered by anyone. In this assumption he was wrong. For he discovered there was no lock on the door, which meant that anyone could enter, hopefully after first knocking.

Molly soon slipped into her original role of Cook/Housekeeper. She knew the dishes, which Abe preferred, but she knew nothing of Ed's. Preferences. He seemed to eat what ever was put in front of him without comment. In fact he spoke very little apart from the usual necessities of 'please and thank you' or a negative shake of the head. Abe seemed happy to ignore his son's morose behaviour, perhaps he was used to it by now. But Molly had been raised by Parents who insisted on good manners however you felt, Consequently after three days of these disjointed replies, Molly Decided that she'd had enough.

As usual, Ed had shut himself unsociably away in the Bunkhouse. Molly washed up the breakfast things, and then drying her hands and taking off her apron she prepared for battle. Marching across the yard to the Bunkhouse, she thumped loudly on the door and waited for a response. But there was none. After a few seconds she thumped once again, more loudly. But still there was no response from inside.

Molly became alarmed, was Ed ill or asleep, but surely if he was either of those, he would have at least answered. But still there was silence. Without stopping to think, Molly grasped the door handle and burst into the room. Imagine her shock when she met an astonished Ed who had just stepped out of the shower, calmly he took a towel and tucked it tightly around his waist. I'm sorry I didn't hear you, as you can see I was in the shower. I gather from your impulsive entry, that you wanted to speak with me. He said. Looking at her enquiringly. Molly blushed with embarrassment and stammered, S-s-s-sorry. I didn't know that you were in the shower. How would you know? Ed asked with an amused smile. Are you going to tell me what you came for, because I would really like to get some clothes on? I'll go! Molly replied, backing towards the door. Come back in five minute, I'll be decent then and you can tell me what it was you wanted to say to me. Ed offered. Molly hurried back to the house, wishing that she hadn't gone to the Bunk House to look for Ed.

When Molly came down to the kitchen next morning, the fire was lit, the kettle was on the hob and a dirty coffee cup was in the sink. Molly began to prepare breakfast for Abe and anyone else who wanted it.

Presently Abe came in, he had been to feed the chickens and look for eggs. He held a blue bowl containing brown eggs. Morning Little Maid, he greeted her, you could have had a lie in. You didn't need to get up so early. There was no sign of Ed, and Molly wondered where he was. He didn't appear for breakfast either.

Abe didn't seem worried that Ed wasn't at the breakfast table. Eventually Molly remarked on his absence. He's probably still asleep, Abe replied. He's up half the night, sometimes all night, and then he sleeps in the day. Well, Molly thought. Abe wanted me to come and see if I could help sort out Ed's problems. Where do I start? And does Ed even want me to try? She thought about this problem for a while discarding several ideas, until she eventually decided to play it by ear and do what she could. After all I'm not a professional counsellor she thought.

Molly had put the dishes in the Dishwasher, put the clothes into the Washing machine and made the beds. What I should really be doing is going to the Bunk House and speaking to Ed. She told herself reluctantly. Then walking across the yard she knocked on the Bunkhouse door. There was no answer. Why am I not surprised? Molly asked herself. And knocked once more. But the door remained closed and no movement could be heard inside the room. Tentatively, Molly opened the door. The room was empty. Drat the man! Where has he gone now? Molly muttered impatiently. Where you looking for me? Ed asked? Suddenly appearing behind her. Molly gave a frightened start. Oh for goodness sake! Do you have to creep about like that she exclaimed. I'm sorry, force of habit I'm afraid, can't get used to living a normal life and not having to watch out for Booby traps and Terrorists. He opened the door and ushered her in, then offering her the only chair he seated himself on the bed. Now what is it you wanted? He asked politely.

What I want, Molly replied sternly, is a straightforward explanation for the reason why, after ignoring me for years, you suddenly sent me a birthday card and a book. Ed looked surprised. The card was because it was your 21st Birthday and the dedication in the book explains the rest. No, I think that isn't the real reason, there is something that you're not telling me and I intend to stay here until you tell me the truth. Molly insisted. Ed looked at Molly's beautiful face and determined little chin, and knew that he would find it difficult to withstand her demands, but he had made up his mind that for her sake he must keep his distance.

Ed was trying to gather his wits together, but he was having difficulty in thinking how to give Molly a convincing answer. I'm Waiting! Molly raised her brows and giving him an expectant look. Ed replied lamely. I thought you would like it. He was playing for time; but he couldn't give her the real reason, although he longed to do so. Molly shook her head. Not good enough try again! She demanded, and she settled herself more comfortably into her chair. Ed wracked his brain to think of an answer that would satisfy her. Thinking to himself, this is worse than being interrogated as a suspected spy. He shook his head, I'm afraid that I don't have an answer, at least not one that I can tell you.

Well I think I know the answer, Molly replied, rising gracefully to her feet, but you will have to tell me in your own good time. But don't wait too long because I have to go back to school at the end of the Vacation. You have three months to think of an answer. Otherwise I will tell you the answer myself. And without another word, she went back to the house, leaving Ed mystified and speechless.

Molly couldn't settle after that unsuccessful interview, and decide to go into town and visit Dolly. She had been searching in the shed for a yard broom, and had found that the cycle was still there. Dusty but still roadworthy. She collected her sun hat from the house and set off to town. The cycle was heavy going and Molly was soon feeling hot and dusty, but she pressed on and was glad to reach the Diner at last.

When she entered, the doorbell tinkled just as loudly as she remembered, but Dolly's cheerful face wasn't behind the counter. A younger model of Dolly greeted her. Molly ordered a cold drink, and asked. Has Dolly retired? No but she usually has a rest in the afternoons after the lunchtime rush. I'm her niece Donna Porter; I'm engaged to Todd Ford at the garage. The girl replied. They exchange news of folk that Molly had known when she had been there before, When Molly had related the saga of how she and Pippa had come to be so far away from Vancouver, Donna had exclaimed, Oh My! I don't think I could be bold enough to do such a prank. It was my sister Pippa who was always the bold one, Molly laughed, and I went along with her mistakenly thinking that I could prevent her from doing anything too audacious. But somehow I could never stop her. Presently Dolly came down to see who was in the Diner, laughing with Donna. She was delighted to find Molly and hugged her warmly, Saying Oh My! What a beauty you've grown into. I always said that you would, and I can see that I was right. Presently Todd came to drive Donna home and Dolly began to lock up. I don't open late now, she explained. Several new Soda bars have opened and they have those nasty noisy Jukeboxes. I can't abide those things. My son Jed say's I should have one, as they're all the 'Rage'. Well let them 'Rage' some place else I don't want them in my Diner.

Todd noticed that Molly had arrived on the heavy old cycle and he offered to take her back to the farm. She gratefully accepted, and Todd loaded the cycle onto the back of his truck. On her return she found that Abe had thoughtfully put the pie that she had left ready, into the oven.

During the night Molly woke, something had disturbed her, it had sounded like an engine, but she turned over and slept again. When she came down in the morning Abe told her that Ed had gone.

Why would he do that? Molly asked, in surprise. He didn't say, Abe replied, only that he couldn't stay here at the moment. It's because of me isn't it? Molly said in distress. I'm sure of it, I could see that he didn't like it when I arrived and his sudden leaving has proved it. I'm so sorry Abe I have driven him away, just as you have got him back after all these years. No, no, Maid, don't you be blaming yourself.

Abe assured her, he's not right yet from his Battle Trauma, he's got a way to go yet before he's really over it.

Ed himself knew that it wasn't the Battle Trauma from which he was suffering, that had made him leave, but something much more difficult to cure, and that was why he'd felt that he had to go. He had gone back to his apartment in Vancouver thinking that he would be unlikely to meet Molly there. But in that he was mistaken, for he had forgotten about his friendship with Nate. And although Nate had told him of his engagement, the name of the girl meant nothing to him for he had never heard of her, or of her association with Molly and her family.

Consequently when Nate invited him to his engagement party, he agreed to attend. Nobody would know him, although he knew that Molly lived in Vancouver. It's a big city, he told himself; I'm not likely to meet her there.

There still remained several more weeks of her school vacation, and Molly decided that she would go home. Abe agreed there was nothing she could do to help Ed even if he were there, and so she reluctantly returned to Vancouver, promising Abe that she would keep in touch.

There was much excitement over Nate and Marcia's Engagement Party. Nate wanted it to be special, and because he had no relatives to invite, he made up for it with friends. Marcia and the three girls went shopping, excitedly trying on so many gowns that they became bewildered, and Dora who had come with them eventually took charge to sort them out. Which she did expertly, having had plenty of practice with Pippa and Molly as teenagers? At last they were all fitted out and returned home tired but satisfied.

CHAPTER TWENTYONE

The party was to be held at a prestigious Hotel. And when the Manning's and friends arrived, they were very impressed, and the ladies were pleased that they had all bought new gowns. It's so easy for men, Pippa had complained, they only have to put on a Tuxedo and comb their hair and they're ready, we have so much to do. Yes but its exciting getting ready, don't you think? Fern replied. I'd rather have a pretty gown than a boring old Tuxedo any day, wouldn't you? The dinner was delicious and beautifully served, and after a few speeches the guests drifted into the ballroom where a small orchestra was playing. No Disco for this Hotel, Gil murmured as he took Fern in his arms to dance.

Ed had been caught up in traffic and had arrived as dinner was being served, he had been placed at a table on the other side of the Dining Hall and had not recognised any of the other guests.

He now stood at the side of the Ball Room, idly watching the dancers, when suddenly he received a shock, for there was Molly, dancing with a tall good-looking man. His dark hair curled attractively and one curl fell across his forehead. Molly smiled up at him, and as he bent his head she whispered in his ear, at his reply she laughed delightedly, and Ed felt his blood boil with envy. That should be me, he thought angrily. And whose fault is it that is isn't. You've only yourself to blame. His conscience told him. He turned away, wishing now that he hadn't agreed to come. And I wouldn't have if I'd know that Molly was going to be here. Well I can't leave so soon, but I won't stay very long he promised himself. Nate had done his best to introduce as many of his guests to each other as possible. But when he introduced Molly to Ed, she said. Oh I know Ed very well, I stayed at his home at the beginning of the School Vacation. Well, I'll leave you two to reminisce, Nate replied moving on to introduce some more folk to each other.

Molly looked at Ed. He didn't look well, as if he was having trouble sleeping. In this she was right, for Ed's dreams were all of Molly, and he couldn't sleep properly because of them, and the worst of it was that he didn't know what to do about it. He knew what he wanted to do but he didn't have the courage to do it.

I'm rubbish at this relationship game he thought. I've spent so much time running from danger that I'm out of touch with normality. Molly had moved on to speak to some other guest that she knew. Pippa noticed Ed, she didn't know who he was but she thought him a.'Dream Boat' Wow! He's something else, she thought, not as handsome as my Nate, but not far off. He doesn't seem to be with anyone. I think I'll team him up with Molly; she's not dancing at the moment. She boldly approached Ed, saying, I wonder if you would mind dancing with my sister, she's rather shy and doesn't have a partner to dance with. As she spoke she was leading him across the room, and halted in front of Molly, who was trying to hide behind a potted Palm. Here we are, Pippa said brightly, Molly this is Ed, and Ed this is Molly. Now enjoy your dance both of you, no good sitting on the sidelines. 'Have fun', she said as she whisked away to introduce a few more people.

Both Ed and Molly stared at each other at a loss for words. Molly was the first to recover. I'm sorry about that, she said. My sister likes to pair people up, and being a nurse she is quite bossy and expects us to do as we're told. In that case we'd better not disappoint her, she might return to check up on us. Ed replied and he indicated that Molly go before him on to the dance floor. He took her in his arms and began to guide her around the Ballroom floor. It was a slow number and Ed held her firmly, Molly didn't draw back as she would have done if it had been a stranger, instead she melted against him. Ed held her closer, but she made no objection and they danced in close harmony for the rest of the dance. When the orchestra began to play another number, instead of letting Molly go to leave the dance floor, Ed held her closer and they continued to dance. Molly closed her eyes and drifted on a cloud. During the evening they spent a great deal of time talking and explaining. Ed told her of the explosion that had caused his trauma and his subsequent nightmares. He told her of his father's devotion to him night after night, sitting with him to calm him down, I've had many Trauma Sessions and they have been a great help to me. He told her. When you came to the Farm I was still having nightmares and so I moved out and came back to my apartment in Vancouver. I wanted to stay and talk to you, but I was ashamed of myself for being so weak. But you weren't weak you were Ill, that's not the same thing. Molly protested. It felt like it to me. Ed replied. I do wish that you had told me all this back in the summer. I would have been able to help you with your physio and relaxation. Don't be too proud in future, I want to help you.

I wanted to tell you how I felt when you came to see me in the Bunk House. But you didn't come back and I thought you had given up on me, he replied. No, it was because I was embarrassed, that was why I didn't say what I really thought, Molly explaimed. I was intrigued to know what it was that you said you knew, but wouldn't tell me he said. I was bluffing Molly told him. I hoped that by saying that I knew, you would believe me and say that you agreed with me. Um! I understand you, I think! Ed replied. In other words you were giving the wrong answer to get the right one from me. But you didn't come back so I wasn't able to give you an answer. Was I?

The orchestra had begun to play another slow number, and Ed stood up, holding out his hand, saying They're, playing another slow number, come and dance, then leading her to the dance floor, he took her in his arms holding her close as they swayed to the music. Another couple on the dance floor were also swaying to the music.

And when the Singer began to sing the words, 'Sooner or later I'm gonna be falling in love with you,' Gil held Fern closer, and murmured, Do you remember this was the first song we danced to, and I told you it wouldn't be he last time, but the first of many. Yes! Fern sighed, it seems so long ago, and so much had happened since then.

Most of it good I hope? Gil asked. Yes, and even the bad parts have just brought us closer together. Fern assured him.

Soon the orchestra was playing The Last Waltz, and then it was a flurry to collect wraps and coats. So many Goodbyes' and 'Lovely to meet you', and 'See you again soon', and everyone then went on their separate ways,

Fern and Gil were the first to leave, for Fern was anxious to get back home. They had left the baby with a baby sitter. And although she was a trained nurse, Fern still couldn't help worrying.

Molly and Ed were loathed to part, and Ed drove slowly. He parked for a while outside the house after Molly's family had gone inside. I don't want to go Sweetheart but I know I must. He said, after they had kissed several times. Stay a little while longer, Molly coaxed. Ed was easily persuaded, and eventually asked, Are you going to marry me? I've never considered marrying anyone else ever since I first met you, so please say Yes! I've wanted to hear you say that, even when we were at the farm but I thought you didn't like me. Molly replied. Ed smiled. If you knew how often I wanted to kiss you then, you would have told me to back off. I was feeling the same. Molly replied. What a pair we are, we've wasted so much time. Well that's fine, now we have an excuse to make up for lost time, Ed replied taking her in his arms once more.

Will I see you tomorrow? Molly asked. Because tomorrow my Dad's two brothers and their wives are visiting, and I'd like you to meet them, Then you will have met all the family and have done it all at the same time. Ed agreed, although he might find it hard, for since his illness he had found it difficult to be in a crowd of strangers. But for Molly's sake he would do anything.

The next day proved to be happy day, for Dora and Phil. Gil's brothers and their wives

Weren't able to visit very often for they both had businesses to run. Both couples had two sons. But the boys were all away at Summer Camp. Dora was disappointed not to see her grandsons, but she was delighted to see the grown ups and hear all the news of their sons. Sue and Jan both congratulated Beth on producing another Grandson for the family. Because they both had boys they had wondered if Fern would manage to break the chain and produce a girl. But it was not to be. Better luck next time. They joked.

After the party and family visits, life seemed quiet and uneventful, and Fern was thinking how pleasant it was. The weather was fine, and her life was ideal. Until she received a letter from England, which set her whole world in a turmoil.

CHAPTER TWENTY-TWO

Bennett had managed to employ a Houskeeker who ignored his tantrums and stayed in the job. Perhaps it was because Mrs, Holt had worked for some years as Matron in a home for delinquent boys. And was used to dealing with temper tantrums. Whatever the reason she remained and life became more comfortable for Bennett. Except for the fact that he still had no Heir. Eventually he decided to apply to a Marriage Bureaux.

At first there was no lack of young ladies applying for such an attractive marriage opportunity. That was until they met Bennett, and after a few samples of his uncontrollable tantrums, they very soon left. They had probably reported their experiences to the Marriage Bureaux, for he was told that they had no young ladies available at the moment. Gradually, Bennett worked his way down the list of Bureaux and soon received the same excuse from all of them. No doubt the word had been passed around amongst them and nobody wanted to risk their reputation by dealing with him.

Only one girl agreed to a second date with Bennett. She was not the type of girl that Bennett would have chosen. On the first occasion, when she had arrived, she had been shown into the Sitting Room, while Mrs.Holt had gone to tell Bennett, of her arrival.

As Bennett entered the room, he discovered the girl looking at the Dresden and Sevres China which she had removed from the glass cabinet, as if she were assessing their value. He hoped he was wrong and ignored the rude behaviour. The evening out, although not a raging success passed without any upsets, and further evenings were arranged.

Bennett began to feel that his goal might at last be in reach, but the best-laid plans often go awry and so it was in his case. Bennett had suggested that perhaps they might get married, and Vanda enthusiastically began to outline her plans for a Grand Wedding and Reception. Bennet pointed out that because this was to be a marriage of convenience there was no call for such an expensive affair. Vanda began to argue and as Bennett's refusals became more adamant, so Vanda's angry insistence became more pressing. Soon they were having a fine royal row and were shouting hysterically at each other, until Bennett went into one of his uncontrollable Tantrums. Vanda had been shouting as loudly as Bennett, so loud had their shouting become that Mrs.Holt, who could hear them from the kitchen came to act as Referee. She intended to send Vanda packing, but as she opened the door and stepped into the room, Bennett, clutching his chest, fell to the floor. Vanda taking fright ran from the room and snatching up her coat as she went, she flung open the front door and fled. While Mrs Holt, did her best to resuscitate Bennett. After a few minutes, she straightened his limbs, and gently closed his eyes. Then she rang for the Doctor, to come and confirm that Bennett was dead. The combination of his heavy drinking and years of continual uncontrollable raging tantrums had damaged his heart and consequently, the last tantrum had been one tantrum too many.

There's some Post for you Honey, Gil said as he laid the letters on the breakfast table, Looks like you've got one from England. Fern picked up the letter eagerly. I hope it's from Tessa she said. But it wasn't Tessa's writing. And she opened it, hurriedly scanning the contents; she gave a shriek, Bennett's Dead! She exclaimed in shock. What! Gil replied, holding out his hand for the letter. Fern dropped down into a chair, for she was feeling weak with shock. Not because she was fond of Bennett, but because she had been expecting to hear that he had successfully married, not that he was dead. There was worse news to come, for the letter was from Bennett's Solicitor, to say that Fern was his Heir. And that Eastleigh House and Estate were now hers, and what did she want him to do about it?

Fern was so stunned that she didn't know what to say, and when she got her breath back her first reaction was to say. I don't want it sell it all! I don't care!. Gil had been reading the long and detailed document which the Solicitor had sent to Fern, Looking up he said sympathetically, Sorry Honey, you can't do that. The whole of the Property is in Trust. I don't understand Fern said in bewilderment, I'm not even a blood relative, how can it be mine? Apparently it was your Stepfather's wish. He guessed that Bennett might not marry, and if that proved to be so, he made arrangements so that the house and land wouldn't be sold off to build dozens of houses as has happened to so many other Estates. He willed it all to you and your Heirs. But I don't want it! Fern repeated her first refusal once more. I'm afraid you're stuck with it Honey, there's nothing you can do. Gil replied. But I don't want to go and live there, Fern sobbed, you know I hated it when I was growing up. Yes, but Bennett wouldn't be there now would he? Gil said. No, but I would feel as if he were there, criticising my every move and decision. You can always put a Manager in to care for it until our Son is old enough, Gil suggested. Don't be too upset Honey, and don't worry we'll work something out. One option would be to employ an Estate Manager. We could go for a holiday each year to keep an eye on things, and also visit Tessa, Bart, the kids, and Bitza. You always loved the beach at Eastleigh and I'm sure that Simon, Marina and Jamie would love it too.

Gil phoned Greg with the news and to ask him for advice. Sorry to involve you in our dilemma. He told Greg, I know nothing about these matters, but you're a lawyer from England so you know the Law, what do you advise? He asked. Don't apologise. Greg said, that's what friends are for. I'm glad to help, after all I wouldn't be here if it weren't for Fern. Leave it with me, I'll do a little digging and let you know what I discover. Two days later, Greg rang them to ask if it were OK with them he would come to the house that evening with his findings and suggestions.

Fern couldn't wait for Greg to come, she felt restless and on edge, after the shock of learning what her Step Father had done. When Greg and Marcia arrived, Fern could hardly wait to hear what Greg had to say.

Firstly, Greg told them. You can't change the Will. But there is nothing to stop you from putting in a Manager to run the Estate and care for the House. The present Manager is willing to stay on until a new Manager has been found and trained. He is coming up to retirement but is willing to do all he can to keep the Estate running smoothly. He had great respect for Mr Dawson Senior who took him on as a boy and feels it is the least he can do, for he has always been grateful for the chance he was given. The House Keeper is also willing to stay until you arrive or even permanently if you require. It's a big house so you will need help. It seems that your stepfather thought more of you than you knew.

When he was making his will the Solicitor had queried his decision to leave the Estate in trust to you. Mr Dawson had replied, 'I wish my son had as much kindness and humanity, as my stepdaughter, the Tenants are all respectful to him, but they all love her.' My wife died giving birth to Bennett, and I'm afraid that I unconsciously blamed him for my sad loss. I was too severe on him I see that now. I sent him away to Boarding School when he was 5 years old, it was too harsh a place for a young child and it turned him into an unfeeling despot, and the only thing that became important to him was the Estate. He was jealous of Fern because everyone loved her and he felt that nobody had ever loved him.

My next suggestion I'm not sure if you will like. Greg said. Marcia and I have talked this over at great length and have decided that I would like to apply for the job as the New Manager, and for us to go and live in Eastleigh House as caretakers and custodians. For a moment there was a shocked silence and then Fern cried. What! Do you really mean it? That's a wonderful idea, but do you both want to go back to England again to live? Yes as a matter of fact we do. Greg replied. I still feel that I'm British not Canadian and I can't seem to change; Marcia loved it in England, and would have stayed if it hadn't been for her fear of Bennett. We neither of us have family here, and now there's nothing stopping us, if you are willing for us to take the jobs

I think it's a fantastic idea, Fern agreed,. Now tell me all you have found out about this strange arrangement by my Step Father, and is it Legal.

Once assured that all was above board and Legal, Fern was pleased for them and wished them every success and happiness, although she was sad to see them go. But we will come and visit once a year she promised.

I didn't know that Greg didn't feel 'At Home 'in Canada. Fern remarked. Just shows you can never tell what other folk are feeling. Gil replied. I'm so pleased that Greg and Marcia were happy to go to Eastleigh; Fern said as they prepared for bed, everything seems to have worked out right. So many Consequences have happened in our lives and all have turned out for the good. Except for Bennett's Consequence, Gil said, he was his own worst enemy. Mine too! Fen declared. Don't bare grudges Honey, Gil replied. It's bad for you and the baby. You don't want a 'Grumpy baby girl' do you? What baby girl? Fern asked, puzzled. 'A Special Order', Gil replied. Switching out the light.

When their twins were laid in her arms, Fern smiled up at Gil, and said teasingly. I did warn you to beware of the consequences when you wish. You wished for a baby girl, and now you have two girls.

Bending down to kiss Fern and the babies. Gil replied. Yes, and I couldn't be happier.

THE END

www.ingramcontent.com/pod-product-compliance
Ingram Content Group UK Ltd.
Pitfield, Milton Keynes, MK11 3LW, UK
UKHW042001230426
12048UKWH00009B/465